WICKED MIDNIGHT

M VIOLET

Cover Design by Maria Christine Pagtalunan (Artscandare Book Cover Design). All stock photos licensed appropriately.

Edited by Kat's Literary Services

Formatted by Champagne Book Design

For information on subsidiary rights, please contact the publisher at authormviolet@gmail.com

Printed in the United States of America

This one's for my mom.
Even though she's not allowed to read it.

A NOTE FROM THE AUTHOR

Wicked Midnight is a dark romance meant for 18+ readers only. This is a short smutty novella based on Cinderella. With situations that not all readers may find comfortable, extreme discretion is advised. Please see the TWs below.

Trigger Warnings

*Graphic sexual scenes
*Graphic language
*Physical assault
*Sexual assault
*Coercion
*Dubious consent
*Non-Consent
*Sex with multiple partners
*Group play
*Blood play
*Knife play
*Bondage
*Submission
*Death of a child (only spoken about)
*Parental abuse
Kinks: choking, spanking, restraints, biting, food play, praise, sex toys, and degradation.

WICKED MIDNIGHT PLAYLIST

cinderella's dead—EMELINE

I am not a woman, I'm a god—Halsey

THE DEATH OF PEACE OF MIND—Bad Omens

Martyr—KiNG MALA

Bejeweled—Taylor Swift

too hot to cry—Nessa Barrett

Where's My love (Sped Up)—SYML

Miracle—Bad Omens

LOVE AND WAR—AVIVA

Sucker for Pain—Lil Wayne, Wiz Khalifa, and Imagine Dragons
(featuring Logic, Ty Dolla $ign, and X Ambassadors)

Vigilante Shit—Taylor Swift

Princesses Don't Cry—CARYS

Fever (feat. Klangstof)—CUT_

White Wedding—Bukola

A Dream Is a Wish Your Heart Makes—Christina Perri

WICKED
MIDNIGHT

CHAPTER 1

In Cinder Falls, Fae princesses were groomed to become queens. But we wielded no power beyond our titles. We were valued for only one thing—mating. A queen couldn't rule without a king by her side. If she was even allowed to rule at all. The thought of some strange Fae man's hands roaming my flesh made me physically sick. Hands that would take away my innocence... I knew this day would come but I wasn't ready.

"*Tallulah*," the queen whined. I hated the way she said my name. It was cold and too formal for a mother's tone. But she *was* my stepmother and her lack of warmth toward me had been there my entire life. My real mother had passed giving birth to me, and my father wasted no time securing a new bride. The new queen raised me at an arm's length away. She controlled the lands, the king, and me. And she'd never let me forget it.

"Yes, Your Highness?" I replied, mimicking her iciness.

"I expect you to honor us tonight. It's a miracle the king is even entertaining this little charade of yours. You're lucky he has a soft spot for you."

The *little charade* she was referring to was the masquerade ball that would decide my fate tonight. How stupid of me to expect my own parents to show an ounce of warmth and compassion.

"Yes, stepmother. I thank the king kindly."

The queen's skirts swished across the marble floor as she pranced around my room. "We expect a choice to be made by the end of the week, Tallulah. Or we'll make it for you. We cannot endure any more shame on our family name."

My stomach twisted in knots. *The shame that she would never let me forget.* "I understand."

This was my last attempt to have some control over who I was to spend the rest of my life with. Was I foolish to think that I could find my soulmate in a crowd full of gold diggers and strangers?

My perfect mate had to be here tonight. He just had to. Otherwise, I might have to spend forever in the missionary position under the sweaty Earl of Wonderland. He had a terrible temper and was the same age as my father. I shuddered at the thought of him touching me.

No. That could not be my fate.

She snapped her fingers, and a shimmery cloud enveloped

me. Goosebumps pebbled my flesh as the queen's Fae magic coated me. I looked in the mirror and gasped.

"*Stepmother*, this is indecent. I am barely covered."

In a flash she was behind me, pulling the strings of my corset so tight I could barely breathe. Her ice blue eyes filled with contempt as she glared back at me.

"*You are a Fae princess*, Tallulah. Don't be such a prude. We need to show your suitors just how valuable you are."

I choked back tears as I took in the full view of the dress she had locked me in. I was encased in pink satin. The straps were thin and hung off my shoulders. The neckline plunged down below my cleavage. The skirts fell to the floor, gathering in bunches like squiggly frosting on a cake. It was exquisite but the slits on either side left me feeling vulnerable and exposed. They hiked all the way up to the top of my thighs.

I lowered my eyes, afraid to meet her expectant gaze. "It's lovely, Your Highness."

She gave the ribbons of my corset one more hard yank before tying them off into a bow behind my back. "And remember, Tallulah, they must look but not touch. No respectable Fae nobleman wants tainted goods."

My cheeks flamed bright red. A mixture of shame and anger coursed through my veins. I was just a token of the crown to them. A piece of property for them to trade as they wished. No one cared about what I wanted. But there was no love between us, so how could I expect her to care about my happiness?

"I have no intention of ruining your special night, stepmother," I snapped.

She flicked her hand and stars filled my vision. My knees buckled. "Don't sass me, young lady!"

I gasped for breath as her magic snaked around my throat. *"Please...* Your Highness."

"You're lucky I need you to look your best tonight." She lowered her hand and the air swooshed back into my lungs.

The dress didn't have a wrinkle on it despite the hard fall, but no doubt my knees were bruised underneath. I could already feel them swelling.

"I meant no disrespect. My apologies, Your Highness."

"Finish getting ready, Princess. Your guards will escort you to the ballroom in an hour." She glided to the door and exited without a sound. I waited until all traces of her magic were gone before exhaling.

Reaching under my skirts, I rubbed at the welts that were forming on my knees. I released my magic through my fingertips, guiding it gently to where it hurt the most. Where the queen's powers were dark and destructive, mine were laced with stars and light. I was a healer. It was as if the gods had given me this gift as recompense for placing me in the hands of monsters.

Within minutes, it was as if the wounds were never there. But the memories of the pain she inflicted never really left me. I gathered my blonde strands into a low chignon and took another look in the mirror. The dress *was* beautiful, and it fit me like a glove. *I just felt so naked.* My breasts were of ample size and this corset had them pushed up so high I could almost rest my chin on them.

Beneath the skirt, I wore only a thin pair of lace panties.

If so much as a gust of wind blew against me, the whole king-dom would see them. No matter how much I tucked and ad-justed, I was exposed in some way.

Tears threatened to fall again, but I held them back. I couldn't risk angering the queen any more than I already had. I wriggled my fingers and watched my bare face transform into full makeup. With pink glittery gloss on my heart-shaped lips and black kohl liner around my eyes, I looked like the ex-quisite princess they all wanted me to be.

A knock on the door came just as I placed the royal crown upon my head. "It's time, Princess."

I sucked in a deep breath and stood in front of my cham-ber doors, willing my trembling hands to still. *This is it, Tallulah. Freedom from this existence… or a life even worse than the one you've been living behind these palace walls.*

All eyes were on me as I sauntered down the grand marble stair-case into the royal ballroom. Lust-filled gasps and satisfied gazes met me with each step I took. Their masked faces unnerved me. They were hidden while I was so exposed, the only one bare and unobstructed. I was on display like a glittering diamond for all the kingdom to feast on.

The crowd parted, making a path for me to walk through. I made my way to the top of the room to where my father and stepmother were seated, taking the chair on the other side of the king. With pursed lips, he simply gave me a nod.

I could never tell if he approved or was disappointed. He was a hard man to read. Our relationship was built on formalities and custom. I think I was just an unhappy reminder of the first queen he loved. He couldn't mask the shame in his eyes when he looked at me.

I shuddered as the breeze from the open windows fluttered through and crawled up my skimpy gown. I resisted the temptation to cast a warming spell over myself. The queen hated when I used my magic in front of her. She said it was tainted. See, I was the only healer in my court. A strain of magic I inherited from my birth mother. The king and queen saw it as a weakness. I couldn't destroy lands or barriers like they could.

And that is why they made sure that no one from my birth mother's court would be in attendance tonight. They wanted their heir to marry a dark Fae like them. In hopes that we would have little dark Fae children to rule one day. But all that mattered to me was a marriage of love and hope. Dark or light… it was unimportant. My future children would be doted on and loved. I vowed they would never know the iciness of this court.

The main chandeliers dimmed, and the room lit up with a thousand twinkle lights, sparkling like fireflies. The orchestra began to play a haunting melody that sent goosebumps over my flesh. Well-dressed Fae men lined up to have their turn at a dance with me.

"Time to earn your place, Tallulah," the queen snapped.

I glanced at my father, looking for some sort of encouragement. *Anything* other than the transactional exchange we usually had. But his gaze remained on the crowd. My heart sank. I nodded at the queen and rose from my royal chair.

Inhaling a deep breath, I stalked to the head of the long line of suitors. The first one took my arm in his and led me to the dancefloor. As he twirled me around the room, the masked faces watched me hungrily.

The night blurred as I changed hands a dozen times. Each one held me a little tighter than the last. A few even rested their hands a little too low for my comfort level. My body was here but my mind was twisting away. Drifting off to another place.

Beads of sweat dripped down my bodice as the music grew more intense. They twirled me faster, harder. I was on the verge of passing out. By the time my twenty-fifth dance was over, I could barely breathe. I didn't care what the king and queen thought, I needed a break.

Maybe this was their intention all along? To dizzy me into a stupor so I wouldn't have a choice but to pick someone fast. If only just to end this incessant pounding in my head. No. I wouldn't let them win.

I turned away from the ever-growing line and decided I would get some air. But as I made my attempt, the next suitor caught my wrist. I groaned as he pulled me to his chest. "Going somewhere, Princess?"

His voice was deep and raspy. It sent a little tremor up my spine. I looked up and met his emerald-green gaze. His mask was jet-black and devoid of any frills. While most of the attendees did their best to outdo each other with glitter, jewels, and rich fabrics, this man dripped in understated elegance.

"I was just about to get some air," I replied.

He cradled my lower back in his palm. Heat radiated from his skin, warming my already fiery flesh. "Good idea. I'll come with you."

I tried to protest but he was already dragging me across

the room toward the veranda. "This is highly unusual, sir. We shouldn't be alone," I called out as he pulled me away from the crowd.

We reached the veranda, but he kept going, leading me down the stone steps and into the garden. My heart raced. "I command you to stop."

The stranger halted and spun around, gathering me in his arms as I stumbled back. "Live in the moment, Princess. You and I both know you seek adventure."

I eyed his lips. They looked soft and full, glistening. *This was indecent.* "Yes, but I shouldn't be out here alone with you."

He tightened his grip on my waist. "Relax… This is your night, Princess. I'm at your mercy. *Command me.*"

Butterflies danced in my stomach while all the dirty things I wanted done to me invaded my mind.

CHAPTER 2

Fireflies flitted around us. The scent of honeysuckle swarmed my senses as the stranger dipped his head to my neck. "What do you dream about, Princess?" he whispered, and his breath tickled my skin.

My heart pounded, throbbing in my ears. "Freedom," I whispered back.

It was only a matter of time before my guards would find me out here, consorting with a strange man without supervision. They would report back to the Queen, and she would punish me. It was a miracle that she was even giving me the option to choose my own mate. Perhaps it was just an illusion. Maybe she put this stranger here just to trick me and rip all of my hope away.

But I could not will myself to step back. Something about him drew me in. I shivered as he pressed his lips to my shoulder. It was gentle and restrained.

"I can show you what it means to be truly free, Princess." He kissed my collarbone. "To lose yourself in the throes of passion. When your body aches from so much want and need that you can no longer contain your desire." The man tugged my head back gently and placed another kiss at the base of my throat.

I let out a soft moan. "We should not be out here, sir. It is unbecoming." And yet I prayed that he wouldn't stop.

He chuckled as his lips made their way up the side of my neck. He kissed my jaw, hungrily, harder than before. "What's *unbecoming* is the thought of your sweet little cunt not getting the release it deserves."

Moisture pooled between my legs. I clenched my pussy as the masked man dragged the tip of his tongue across my jaw. When he got to my chin, he took it into his mouth and sucked.

Fuck.

I had touched myself before but these sensations he was invoking were entirely new. My body tingled as if sparks of electricity zapped through me. I knew the release he was speaking of. I had given it to myself on many a late night. But I couldn't help wondering what it would feel like if someone else were pulling the strings…

I whimpered as he nipped his teeth on my bottom lip. "Tulip…, my princess. My little flower. I want to see how sweet you taste when I spread you open…"

Tulip? My cheeks burned. Heat flooded every inch of me.

What in the world was happening? I could barely breathe. I was completely and utterly entranced by this man. Was this magic?

I straightened and stepped back. A cool breeze swept in between us. "You are out of order, sir."

The man was unfazed. A smirk pulled at the corners of his mouth. "Do you think you're going to be able to choose your mate, *your king*, just based on his ability to waltz? Don't fool yourself, Princess. When the music stops, and the crowds have gone... the only thing that will make you feel free... *is this*."

He held me tight to his chest. Before I could protest, he planted his lips on mine. I moaned into him as his tongue twirled around my mouth, my back arching as his fingers traced the edges of my corset. *I was in so much fucking trouble.*

"Am I right, Tulip... or shall I stop?" His fingertips lingered on the top of my bodice.

"Why do you call me that?" I breathed between kisses.

"Because you are my little flower, and I want every fucking drop of your delicious nectar." He dipped his fingers inside my corset, skimming my nipple.

I bit my lip to stifle a scream. Fuck, it felt so good to be touched by someone. My breath hitched as he pinched my nipple between his fingers.

"Do you like that, Princess?"

I nodded. "Yes," I rasped.

He chuckled again as he pushed me back against the trellis, trapping me inside a wall of flowers. Every exotic scent surrounded me like a sea of perfume and desire. The soft petals caressed my back and neck as he pressed into me.

He moved to my other nipple, rubbing it back and forth

11

between his fingers. I gasped as he sucked on the other one. Stars exploded in my vision as he worked both in an agonizing rhythm. The tingling increased between my thighs.

"Oh, fuck…"

A crisp wind shocked my skin as he pulled my corset open. But it was instantly warmed by his palm on my breast. He began circling his tongue around my nipple. The cool air whipped in between his lips and my stiff peaks, sending shivers up my spine. I sank farther back against the trellis as he rolled the length of his tongue over my entire breast.

"So beautiful, Tulip. You're fucking perfect."

A sensation was building between my thighs, moving to my nub, and shooting tingles to a spot deep within my pussy. And he wasn't even touching me there. *How is this happening?*

I started to cry out, but he covered my mouth. "Shhh…"

An explosion erupted in my nub, and I clenched. Wave after wave of pleasure rolled through me as he clamped his lips around my nipple, sucking and gently scraping his teeth across my swollen flesh.

Sweat beaded down my back as I panted. He withdrew his mouth, and we locked eyes as I came. I had no idea that it could happen this way. Without even touching me down there. It was raw and unsettling, and I loved every minute of it.

Without warning, the masked man slipped his hand under my skirt and swiped at my soaking wet thighs. He brought his finger to his mouth and sucked. A moan escaped him. "The sweetest fucking nectar I've ever tasted."

"Take off your mask," I rasped.

He licked his finger clean and chuckled. "Some other time,

Princess… But I will claim the rest of you soon. I can promise you that."

Before I could even catch my breath, he was gone, disappearing into the night. Into the shadows. And I was left alone in the garden, a wet shivering mess.

I roamed the gardens, searching for him. I had to know his name. His face.

If I was going to go back into that dreadful ball, under the queen's watchful eye, then I had to see him one more time. How could he make me come undone in such a way and then just leave me here breathless?

Turning the corner down another row of rose bushes, I spotted him. He sat on a stone bench, still like a statue. Those green eyes flickered hungrily in my direction. With the moonlight shining down, his chiseled features were pronounced more prominently. His lips looked fuller. A little whimper escaped my lips.

"Come closer, Princess. Now is not the time to be coy." His voice was a little deeper now, raspier.

I inched toward him. "I thought you left me in the garden. What game are you playing sir?"

The man licked his lips. "My favorite kind… The kind where we both win. Now, come here."

I glanced back toward the party, debating on turning back before this man did something so indecent, it would tarnish my image forever. And yet as I looked deep into his eyes, I found myself falling under his spell.

"What do you want from me?" I asked as I stood over him.

He slid his hands through the slits of my skirt, his fingers dangerously close to my throbbing nub. "To feel your slick wet cunt against my face."

Oh, gods.

No one has ever dared spoken to me that way before. What shocked me most was how much I liked it.

I trembled underneath his touch, allowing him to move his hands up my thighs. He tugged at the edges of my panties, tracing my slit over the fabric with his thumb. "Just as I suspected... *soaking wet.*"

I moaned softly as he drew circles around my nub, applying light pressure. I grasped his shoulders to steady myself upright. I was losing control, drowning in the warmth that spread throughout my folds like wildfire.

"Yes, Princess, breathe into it. I knew you'd like that. I want to taste you on my tongue," he rasped.

I closed my eyes and rocked into him. He pushed the slit of my skirt to the side and pulled my panties down. Losing all my sense of reason and decency, I stepped out of them. He guided one of my legs up until my heel rested on the bench.

I gasped as he inched his tongue slowly inside me, then out. "*Delicious...*"

He peeled my sopping wet folds back with his fingers and flicked his tongue against my clit. "What are you doing to me?" I panted.

I dug my fingers into his hair as he devoured me, wanting so desperately for this moment to never end.

"I'm opening you up, Princess. So I can break you."

The sound of boots crunching in the grass, snapped me

out of my reverie. I jerked my head toward the garden. "Wait," I breathed. "Someone's coming."

"Oh, you will be coming that's for sure." The man snickered.

I stilled his head. "No. *Someone* is coming."

He licked his lips as he pulled my panties back up. "You've been gone too long, Princess. The guards must be looking for you."

Disappointment flooded me. My pussy still tingled from his touch. I wanted him to finish so badly. But the queen would lock me in the dungeon until my wedding day if they found us out here.

I nodded. "Who are you?"

His green eyes darkened. "I'll see you soon, Princess."

"Where in the name of the gods have you been, Tallulah?" The Queen whisper-yelled as I returned to my seat on the throne.

"I stepped out for some air. Forgive me." I folded my hands in my lap to keep from fidgeting.

She raised an eyebrow in my direction. "Why are your cheeks flushed?"

Fuck. "Oh, are they? Must have been from the walk back. I did hurry to get back here."

The queen did not seem convinced, but she let it go. "When you have regained your composure, make the rounds through the ballroom. There are still many suitors who have not yet had the pleasure of your time."

A little trickle of relief spooled through me. "Yes, stepmother."

But it was short-lived.

"And Tallulah, pull another stunt like that again and I will have you betrothed to whom I choose by morning."

I gave her a bow before moving past her and every nerve in my body prickled. A subtle flicker of magic flashed in her eyes. A reminder of her power and how she would yield it against me if I pissed her off.

Working my way through the party, stopping to chat here and there with the occasional nobleman, I realized that this whole charade was a joke. The stranger from the garden was right. How could I possibly choose my future mate just from a waltz or one conversation? This was only stalling the inevitable—that I would be chained to a man I barely knew for the rest of my life.

But if I chose someone like *him*... I shivered at the memory of his lips on my breasts. The way his tongue darted over my nipples with such precision and appetite. As if his mouth was made to please only me.

I had to find him again.

With a quick glance to the throne chairs, I could see that the queen was preoccupied with a slew of guests, lining up to pay their respects. This was my chance.

As the music intensified, almost mirroring my desperation and urgency, I combed the ballroom for my mystery man. It was dark in the garden, and he was masked, but I don't think I could ever forget his eyes. They were as green as the Cinder Falls sea. His gaze would haunt me always. As well as his mouth, his raspy voice, his soft fingers...

I had to get out of my head and let my body guide me.

It was a risk to leave the queen's sight again, but I had to be sure this man hadn't left. I had been evading the guards and her ever since I was a kid. When I was sure no one was looking, I slinked up the stairs, holding fast to the wall and out of the line of fairy lights.

There would be no one up here. The guests were indulging in all of our families fineries on the main level. But if my mystery man was as sly as I thought he was, he very well could be wandering these very halls.

After searching all the unlocked rooms and finding no one but the occasional maid who'd come to retrieve more linens, my heart sank. Our palace was packed full of people, but up here, I was searching for a ghost who I'd most likely never see again. And I never felt more alone.

I let out a sigh upon entering the library, the stacks putting me at ease as always. Whenever my world became unbearable, I'd come in here and get lost in somebody else's. I fingered the spines as I passed them, relishing the feel of smooth leather on my skin. The rich smell of parchment invaded my senses as I took in deep breaths, willing myself not to cry.

The beginning of a winter storm was taking its roots outside. I went to the window and looked out toward the garden. It was empty. No trace of my mystery man.

"Hiding from your own party, Princess?" His raspy voice cut through the silence like a sliver of hope.

I kept my gaze forward. Was it really him? His voice was similar but with more edge to it. "I was looking for someone."

17

A draft crawled up my skirt, indicating the man had moved closer. "And did you find him?"

A fluttering stirred in my belly. I was alone again with this stranger. It made me feel vulnerable and scared and a little bit unhinged.

"I don't know. I think so… but you sound different." I was afraid to turn around for fear that any sudden movement would scare him off again.

The man stood so close now I could feel his breath on the back of my neck. With my face pressed to the window, he hiked up the hem of my skirt. My breath fogged on the glass as he curled his fingers around my thigh and squeezed.

"I'm still sticky… from the garden," I breathed.

He snickered and circled his free arm around my waist, pulling me flush against him. "Do you like being treated like a whore, Princess?"

Oh, shit.

CHAPTER 3

I shuddered as his fingers inched further up my thigh. "I'm *not* a whore. How dare you?" Despite my predicament, my embarrassment was quickly turning to desire. This man smelled like ache. Like lust and power and sex. Like an animal in a gentleman's suit.

His hold around my middle tightened. "Admit you like it. Say it, or I will stop and leave you panting in your own juices, unfulfilled."

He wouldn't, would he?

I had no idea what agony truly felt like until tonight. I needed release. Again. Needed something I'd never had before.

The window was cool against my cheek, soothing me as my pussy tingled in anticipation. "Y-yes," I stammered.

The man slipped his hand inside the back of my panties, grabbing a fistful of my ass. "Yes, what? I want to hear you say it."

I scraped my teeth against my lower lip, aching for him to slide his hand lower. I was soaked through. "Yes, I... I like it."

He growled and rammed against me, pressing his hard cock into my lower back. "You like what? *Say it.*"

Fuck. I needed him to touch me. "I like being treated like a whore... *Please.*"

He snickered and slowly slid his hand down the slit of my ass.

I gasped as he raked his fingers underneath and up the front of my pussy. The window creaked under my grip as he reached farther up to find my throbbing clit. His muscled forearm flexed against my ass as he held me in place while I straddled it.

"Gods, you're dripping. Such a good little whore. Gonna give me every fucking drop, aren't you?"

I whimpered, unsure of what to say. I just didn't want him to stop.

"You've never been touched like this before, have you? And that silly little nipple twist in the garden doesn't count." He breathed in my ear, and it tickled every nerve in my body.

Sweat beaded down my back. A surge of shame flooded me. *It was him.* It had to be. But something in him was more feral this time. Like I had awoken something in him.

"Answer my question. Has anyone touched you like *this* before?" He pinched my nub between his fingers.

Fuck, that felt good. This was different from the garden.

Amidst the flower beds and leaves, he had been gentle and

sweet. I couldn't gather my words. Couldn't do anything except shake my head.

"Well, you're in trouble now, Princess, because I'm no charming prince. I'm a fucking monster."

My breath hitched as he shoved a finger deep inside my pussy. I trembled and clenched around him, consumed by every spark of pleasure that rippled through me. This wasn't the same as when I'd touched myself. When I explored the soft folds of my own sex.

No.

This was primal, brutal, and unforgiving. He flicked his fingers inside me, violently, and I hungered for more.

My nipples swelled beneath my corset, aching to be set free. I clung to the window, pressing against it for dear life. For fear if I turned around the spell would be broken, and he'd be gone.

"Am I about to pop your cherry, Princess? Will I get to taste the sweet mix of blood and cum on my fingers?"

Oh, gods.

His fingers curled deeper, hitting a spot so tender, my knees buckled. I pressed my open lips to the glass, my breath fogging it instantly.

What has gotten into me? I had now let this masked stranger defile me three times. "I am not myself today," I murmured.

"You are more yourself than you've ever been." He yanked my head back and growled into my ear. His tone was dark, feral, and ferocious. "And I own that part of you now."

He plunged his tongue into my mouth, and I moaned, his vicious kiss sparking that final push over the edge. And what fluttered through me next was an explosion unlike any I'd ever known.

A cry I did not know I possessed ripped out of me. He untangled his hand from my hair and clamped it tight over my lips to quiet me. While the music from the ball echoed through all the rooms, it was not loud enough to drown out my frenzy.

A fire in my belly spread deep down between my thighs. I clenched my pussy around his fingers as the tingling turned to a chaotic climax I couldn't get ahead of. My legs shook with adrenaline, pleasure, buckling as I struggled to not fall to my knees.

My hips jerked, an involuntary reflex, as he pressed his palm hard against my mound. I couldn't breathe. His lips and tongue replaced the hand covering my mouth, his kiss stealing the air from my lungs. Panting, almost to near convulsions, he pressed me hard against the window.

With his fingers still inside me, soaking in my cum, he whispered, "Something for you to remember when you're bored and lonely and have long since grown tired of this place… *You're welcome, Princess.*"

My head was spinning. Dizzy. Drunk on lust. I whimpered as he slipped out of me and backed away. A chill ran up my spine in the absence of warmth from his muscular chest.

As I turned to face my defiler, he shrank back into the shadows even more. The moonlight trickled in between us like a barrier I couldn't breach.

Breathless, I clamored for words. "What… who are you?"

His lips parted, a deviant smirk following as all the clocks in the palace chimed in unison. "It's midnight. I have to go."

"Wait," I plead in a panic. This man just touched me in

ways that I didn't even know I could fantasize about, let alone experience. "Tell me your name. I command you."

I shouldn't have said that. But I was getting desperate to keep him here. And yet I think I just scared him away.

The man arched an eyebrow, his mask lifting slightly. He snickered. "I'm not under your command, Princess."

Footsteps marched through the hallways. Foot soldiers looking for their princess, no doubt. The clocks chimed louder.

My thighs were soaked in my own juices. I clenched them together, still tingling. I wanted more. The man chuckled, noticing my arousal. He stalked back over and pressed his fingers to my lips. "Suck."

I drew in a sharp breath as we locked eyes. *As green as the Cinder Falls Sea.* "Excuse me?"

He pinched my lower lip. "Open your dirty mouth and suck."

This feels… naughty.

But I didn't want him to leave yet. As I parted my lips, he forcefully shoved both of his fingers inside. Tasting myself on his thick fingers made me wet again.

He watched me with a ferociousness through the mask as I sucked as hard as I could, twirling my tongue around and around, wanting to consume every bit of salt from his flesh.

My nipples pebbled as he pumped them in and out. I clasped his wrist between my palms, clinging to him as he finger fucked my mouth.

Shadows flickered in my peripheral, shapes and figures organizing outside the doors. "Princess! Are you in there?"

I gasped as the man lurched away from me. "Good luck on your upcoming nuptials, Princess."

What the hell? I was getting blown off again?

The soldiers banged against the door. I jerked my head in their direction for a split second and when I turned back, the mystery man was gone. Vanished.

A cold chill settled into the room from an open window. I rushed to it and looked out. I scanned the grounds for any sign of him but saw nothing but trees and grass and moonlight.

Holy... fuck.

I straightened my dress, readjusting my panties, and smoothed out my hair. The guards' impatience grew as they rattled against the door. I groaned and started to walk over when a gleam of metal caught my eye on the floor.

I reached down to find a single cuff link with a raven engraved into it. I knew this sigil. It belonged to House Frost. Their estate was only a few towns over. I grinned. He wasn't getting away from me yet.

The banging grew louder.

"I'm coming," I yelled out.

I threw open the doors and came face to face with the queen. "We've been looking for you for quite some time, Tallulah."

She eyed me carefully, taking stock of every detail of my being. She always noticed things that others did not. A disapproving snarl settled onto her face. "Who was in here with you?"

"No one, Your Highness. I was just taking a quiet moment," I prattled.

She looked down her nose at me. "Another quiet moment? Don't lie to me, child. *I can smell a man.*"

My knees began to shake. I locked them together. I couldn't show her any fear. "You have quite a few of them standing behind you." I nodded to the six guards surrounding us.

"Are you sassing me, young lady?" She roared.

I flinched as she raised her hand, the sharp edge of her magic stopping mere inches away from my face. I shook my head in protest. "Never, my queen. I meant no disrespect. I've been alone this whole time. I swear of it."

I held my breath while I waited for her to punish me. To bring me to my knees.

"Get back downstairs. There are suitors you still haven't danced with."

I nodded. Clenching the cuff link inside my palm, I shuffled past her before she could change her mind.

I spent the rest of the night doing as I was told. Until two o'clock in the morning, I danced. With so many Fae men, I lost count. Each one more boring than the last. The only hope I clung to was finding my mystery man tomorrow.

If only just to tell him he was wrong. I refused to spend my life with a man I grew tired of. Refused to live a life of boredom and loneliness.

Tonight I was stuck in this prison. But tomorrow… I had to find *him*.

CHAPTER 4

I tucked my hair inside my hood and charted a path to the stables. The chill before the dawn was crisp and fresh. It was my favorite time of day. The night had gone, but the sun hadn't yet risen. Even the crows and owls still slept soundly in their nests. It was chilly but refreshing. And after my hedonistic behavior from last night, I needed a sharp wind to cool my feverish skin.

The storm had passed, leaving a clean scent over the grounds. I glanced up at the clear sky, sighing in relief as I couldn't spot a dark cloud in sight. It would make for an easier journey.

House Frost was only a half a day's ride. I could make it there and back with my newly betrothed by sundown. By the time the queen learned of my absence, it wouldn't matter. I will have made my choice. And my father, the king, had made such a public spectacle of my courtship, that he would have to keep his word.

Soon I would be free.

I galloped through the Cinder Falls countryside, my stomach in knots. What if my mystery man refused my hand? It was uncommon for a Fae man to refuse a royal but this one was different. There were many sides to him. He didn't seem the least bit interested in sticking around. What did I know about love and sex anyway? Until last night, the only fingers that had been inside me were my own.

Perhaps the masked man was indulging in a night of fun and would want nothing more to do with me. He did wish me luck on my upcoming nuptials. Or maybe he was just convinced I would choose someone else. I was starting to feel sick thinking about it. I hadn't even stopped to consider that this man may not want to marry me.

The familiar terrain of my family's estate began to fade as I crossed over into the common lands. The estates were smaller, but luxurious for they were still nobility, yet they lacked the grandeur of our royal palace.

The sky began to darken again, the clouds graying and twisting into brutal shapes. A cold chill whipped through the wind like a bad omen. It looked and felt as if at any second the sky would split open and drench the entire world in a heavy rain. I should have known that the storm was far from over.

My horse's hooves echoed the thumping of my heart as we raced forward. Morning was creeping up, but the darkness remained. These lands felt cursed to never see sunlight. It had been many years since I'd traveled through here and it seems I'd forgotten just how cruel the elements could be. Without the comfort of my royal carriage, I was exposed and vulnerable to every single touch of winter.

I dug my heels in and pressed on. It was too late to turn back. The queen would soon discover I was gone and for sure lock me in the dungeon again to teach me a lesson. Just like she did when my half-brother died. She would always blame me for it no matter what I did to convince her otherwise. I couldn't really blame her. Emmanuel should have been king. And now they were stuck with only me.

I spotted House Frost in the distance. It reared out from between the trees, a stone and iron monstrosity of a house with barred windows and black spires that looked ready to be impaled upon.

The thick iron gates sat ajar as if they were expecting company. As I rode through, the air seemed to chill even more. The wind whipped ferociously around me, flapping at my ears. Even my horse tensed as he slowed his canter.

I reached forward and stroked his mane. "It's all right, Wraith, we're almost there."

The animal neighed as if he understood me. Maybe he did. I was Fae after all, and magic slid through my veins alongside my blood.

The grounds were eerily quiet. There were no guards or footmen. Not a single soul seemed to stir. I dismounted Wraith and tied him to a nearby tree. As I walked away a single raven squawked in the distance. Shivering, I pulled the edges of my cloak tight to my chest. A twinge of guilt sliced through me as I left him there alone.

The front door was twice my height, painted black, and covered with moss. With trembling fingers, I reached for the silver door knocker and rapped it gently. The sound echoed through the trees, shattering the silence.

What am I doing out here? This was madness. For all I knew that man could have stolen the cuff link. A sickening feeling twisted in my gut as I realized I could be walking into a trap. The Frost family hadn't made any appearances at court in ages. This could all be some sinister plot to imprison the future queen of Cinder Falls.

Fuck.

I spun around and started back toward Wraith. But he wasn't there. My heart hammered. Oh no. No, no, no. My knees began to buckle as I struggled for air, panic washing over me. *Where was my horse?*

A loud creak echoed behind me.

I spun back around.

Every nerve in my body prickled as the black door inched open. It was moments like these that made me wish I had been born with darker magic.

I held my breath as a figure stepped out.

"To what do we owe this pleasure of your visit, Princess?" A tiny old woman with silver hair and gray eyes stepped out.

My chest heaved as I drew in a sharp breath. The cold wind had whipped my hood back and was making its way into my bones. I was frozen, light-headed, and aching from the ride. Fear held me in place like quicksand.

"Where is my horse?" I stammered. "He was just there a second ago."

The old lady smiled sweetly at me. "Come inside, dear. You'll catch a nasty cold out here."

Fuck. Did I really have a choice?

"My horse, lady, where has he gone?" I persisted.

"Well, to the stables out back, of course. He will be warm and well fed," she cooed.

Something was so strange about this place. "But how? He was tied to that tree. I saw no one come to fetch him."

"They all know the way, my dear. Horses are smart creatures. Now come, please. We are so honored to have you as our guest."

I looked back between the door and the tree, not convinced that my horse untied himself and made his own way to a stable that he had never seen before.

But it was freezing, and she seemed harmless. I would make something up about why I was here, retrieve Wraith, and get back to the palace as fast as possible. Perhaps I could dissuade the queen from punishing me somehow.

I nodded and followed the woman inside. Butterflies swam in my belly as the thick black door closed behind us, trapping me inside with whatever lived here. But I was hit by an instant warmth. A fire blazed in the hearth and the air smelled of sugar and honey.

The old woman gestured for my cloak. "I am Lady George, my dear. I have worked for House Frost since I was a girl your age. I look after the lords of this house too. Ever since their parents died, I have been all they have. It is so nice to have another woman here."

Lords? As in more than one?

"Thank you for your kindness, Lady George. I won't be staying long. I just wanted to return something of yours and then I'll be on my way."

I glanced around nervously, waiting for the lords to reveal themselves.

She placed my cloak on an iron hook by the fire and beckoned me over. "Well, that is very kind of you, Princess. I'm sure the lords will be most pleased."

The gathered skirts of my brown riding dress puffed up around me as I sank into one of the cushioned chairs in front of the hearth. My skin tingled as the heat chased away the chill. "I'm sorry, but how many Frost lords are there? I believe we have only seen one at court."

Lady George chuckled. "How peculiar," she squeaked. "No, Princess, there are two lords of House Frost. And then there's—"

"George, you didn't tell us we had a guest." Black hair. Green eyes. It was him.

I stood abruptly and smoothed out my skirts. "Forgive the intrusion, Lord Frost, I just came to return something. Were you the one who attended my betrothal ball?"

"Please, call me Bronte," he drawled. Bronte licked his lips. "I did. It was... enchanting."

My throat bobbed as the memory of his lips on my body sprang forward. "Ah, well you seemed to have dropped your cuff link on your way out." I retrieved it from my bosom and held it up.

"They really do need to put pockets in dresses, don't they, Princess?" Another man entered the room. He was equally gorgeous with that same black hair and those piercing green eyes. They looked almost identical.

"And you are?" I rasped.

He crossed over to the hearth and rested his arm across the mantle. The flames danced in his eyes like the devil. "Ramsay Frost. At your service. Well, that is if you were satisfied with my services last time."

I swallowed hard as I felt the flushing in my cheeks rise. Lady George averted her eyes to the floor and began humming a strange tune.

"You were at the ball as well?" I stammered.

Ramsay's gaze traveled down the length of my body. "I think you know that I was."

So my mystery man was Ramsay. I think. Or was it Bronte?

I held the cuff link away from me as if it would bite. "Which one of you dropped this?"

"I did," they both said in unison.

I looked back and forth between them, confused. "Well, which is it?"

Bronte plucked it out of my hand. "It's definitely mine."

"How can you be so sure, brother? That looks like my cuff link." Ramsay snatched it from Bronte.

This was impossible. The more they toyed with me, the more I wanted to run out of here. And yet being near them, remembering how close I came to the edge last night... I wanted to feel that way again.

But how was I supposed to choose when one of them was clearly lying?

"Look, I have less than a week to choose a husband, a future king, or one will be chosen for me. Whichever one of you dropped this... will return with me to the palace and marry me."

Lady George jumped from her chair and clapped her hands together. "Oh my! Well, this is wonderful news. Now, quit fooling about, boys and fess up. Which one of you dropped it?"

"It's my cuff link," a new voice chimed in. "But it doesn't matter. None of us are interested in playing royal house with you, Princess."

His eyes were just as green but full of menace. My heart fluttered as he stared daggers at me.

I turned to Lady George. "I thought you said there were only two lords of this manor." What in the hell was going on here?

The new mystery man snickered. "That's because I'm not a lord. But I live here just the same."

"*Oh*, you're the bastard..." I murmured.

"Careful, Princess. I don't feel the need to maintain social graces as much as my brothers do."

I was mortified. "Oh, no. I-I didn't meant to insult you. I just meant..."

He sneered, pulling his lips up into a wicked snarl. And yet it made him look even more beautiful. "I know exactly what you meant."

This was all beginning to seem foolish and pointless. I had

not thought this out clearly. And now here I was alone with an old woman and three devilishly handsome yet troublesome Fae men.

I lifted my cloak from its hook and quickly wrapped it around my shoulders. "I think there has been some sort of mis-understanding. I have done my duty of returning the cuff link, whomever that may belong to, but now I must leave. Thank you for letting me warm up by the fire."

"But the fun hasn't even started yet, Princess," Ramsay drawled.

"No, it hasn't." The bastard fingered the edges of my cloak.

I lifted my chin, forcing myself to meet his feral gaze. "I didn't catch your name, sir."

A flicker of something carnal flashed in his eyes. "Shadow." He leaned over me and whispered in my ear, "But I think I like hearing you call me sir."

I clenched my thighs together as his breath tickled my ear like a lullaby I'd heard before.

CHAPTER 5

"You must stay here until the storm clears. It is not safe for you to ride back in these conditions, my dear."

"*Stay* here? That is highly inappropriate." I could only imagine the look of fury on the queen's face when she did not find me in my chambers in the morning.

The woman had kind eyes, and no doubt meant well but suggesting I, the future queen of Cinder Falls, spend the night in a house with three single and ridiculously handsome Fae men, was preposterous. If my stepmother doubted my purity before…

"Not at all, Princess. I will set you up in our finest room. You will have plenty of privacy. My boys like to have their fun, but they *are* gentleman."

If she only knew how one of them had their fingers inside me just last night, she might rethink that.

I glanced out the window just as the rain drove down harder. "I don't know. My stepmother will…" I couldn't even finish the sentence. I didn't know what the queen would do to me if I didn't return tonight. But it would be painful I was sure of that.

Lady George nudged me toward the sitting area. "I'm sure the queen would not want her only heir to be wandering in the dark like a drowned rat. I insist you stay, Princess. I know you will find everything you need here to be comfortable."

The queen would also prefer that I wasn't her *only* heir. And so would I actually. The pressure to marry wouldn't exist. Besides, Emmanuel had been more fit to rule anyway.

Lady George didn't know the queen the way I did. Her royal highness would rather me perish in a storm than think my innocence was in question.

But what choice did I have? Lady George was not going to let me go. I had come here without my guards and my horse was already exhausted from the journey over. I was half a day's ride from the palace in decent conditions.

"Alright, but just for tonight. I will ride out first thing in the morning."

Lady George clapped her hands together in delight. "Of course, Princess. Now let me show you to your room so you can freshen up. Supper will be ready in an hour. You must be famished."

My stomach grumbled as soon as she mentioned it. But the thought of dining with all three of these men was unsettling.

And yet I couldn't deny I was hungry for something else. The one who had defiled me last night was in this house. I ached to come undone against him again.

If I could just figure out which one, I could make my proposal, and return with him. They would surely not refuse me. And then the queen would have no choice but to grant me my freedom.

Lady George led me to what was to be my room for the night, and I was grateful when she left me to get ready. So many servants doted on me at the palace. I never had a moment to myself.

I looked around the quaint but stately room and let out a sigh of relief. The four-poster bed was draped in lavender silks. Across the room, sat a cozy stone hearth, a fire already blazing in it. A pile of white furs splayed out in front of it. Soft enough to tempt me to strip down and roll around on them. The delicate windows were framed with light blue velvet drapes. Everything about this room was inviting. It was as if a sea of winter had bathed it in frost and fire.

I stood in front of the dressing mirror and took in my appearance. I had left the palace in one of my more modest gowns. But now that I had a plan to draw the deviant out, I would have to make myself look more alluring. I would make it impossible for him to resist me.

With a flick of my fingers, I conjured up a new dress. My skin shimmered as the fabrics fell away from me and new ones emerged.

I took a deep breath and gazed at those light blue velvet drapes, envisioning them wrapped around me. A shade of blue that reminded me of old traditions and ancient Fae gods. As I immersed myself in this vision, my magic threaded through me.

A satisfied smirk settled on my lips as I gazed at myself in the mirror. The sleeves were long and velvety and fit me like a glove. But the open neckline plunged deep down into a V shape, gathering to a point just above my abdomen. The back of the gown pooled out behind me, bustling at the hips into heavy skirts that cascaded down like a waterfall. The front, however, was open and the inside fabric covered me only to the middle of my thighs.

I snapped my fingers and gave myself white knee-high stockings, held up by silver threads that weaved into my ruffled panties. The final touch, a pair of blue satin high-heels, befitted with silver buckles.

With my pale blonde hair down in loose waves and my makeup dewy and soft, I looked innocent and indecent at the same time. A delectable vision, worthy of a true Fae princess.

Now… let's see which one of them will break first.

Three sets of emerald-green eyes flickered as I made my entrance, hungry for more than the delectable roast that Lady George had placed on the center of the table. The rich scent of salty meat mixed with lavender, fresh leaves and soil from the open window, heavy musk, vanilla, and Fae blood, assaulted my senses, nearly knocking me to my knees.

Ramsay snickered at my fumble. "All dressed up and nowhere to go, Princess?"

"I think she looks absolutely divine, brother." Bronte stood and pulled out a chair for me to sit down.

My heart skipped a beat as Shadow's gaze burned into me. He watched every move I made as if he were memorizing them.

I nodded politely at Lady George, who stood to the side, and took my seat across from the three raven-haired deviants. "You won't be joining us, Lady?" I asked, torn between wanting her to stay as a buffer, and thrilled that I might finally be alone without supervision for once.

"Oh no, dear. I never dine with the lords. I'll take my supper in the kitchen as always. Please help yourself to as much as you like." She winked and filled my crystal goblet with dark red wine.

I nearly fell out of my seat. Was she still talking about the food? It couldn't be that obvious. "You are too kind, Lady. Thank you for a lovely supper. It smells delicious."

"Yes, *it* does," Shadow murmured.

As Lady George left the dining room, my breath seemed to fly away with her. "Gentleman." I gave them each a slight nod before placing a gold brocade napkin over my lap.

My courage was beginning to falter as all three of them eyed me like a hungry pack of wolves. Perhaps I should have chosen something less revealing to wear…

We ate in silence, the tension weaving in and out of the room like a thick fog. But their eyes never left me. There was a darkness surrounding each and every one of them. Even Bronte, who seemed the gentlest, still had an underlying air of mischief about him.

At first, I was sure that my mystery man from the ball was Shadow. But now, sitting before them, I was confused. Each one of them felt familiar to me. It was hard to discern as they all looked very much alike, and their scents mingled like fragments of the same whole.

As I finished my wine, Bronte quickly stood to pour me another. "Thank you."

Ramsay slid his chair around the table until he was at my side. He ran his fingers across my shoulder. "Why have you really come here, Princess?"

Heat flooded my cheeks. "To return your cuff links, as I said. And to determine which one of you dropped them at the ball."

"You're asking the wrong questions, Princess," Shadow snapped.

He looked at me with such malice in his eyes. It was infuriating. "Oh? And what should I be asking then?"

Ramsay chuckled as he slid his hand around to the back of my neck and squeezed. "You want to know which one of us defiled you."

"Afraid your innocence might be in question, Tulip?" Bronte chimed in.

I gasped. He called me that in the garden.

Shadow moved his chair to the other side of me. "The question isn't who had his hands all over you… *inside* you. No, Princess. The question you should be asking yourself is *how many times* did each one of us defile you."

I glanced across the table at Bronte for clarification,

but his eyes had darkened just as his brothers'. "I... I don't understand."

"I think you do, Princess," Ramsay hissed. "You see... those cuff links belong to all of us."

Bronte leaned forward, taking my hands in his. "We share everything."

My breath hitched as Shadow's lips grazed my ear. "And now, we're going to share you."

Oh, fuck. *All three of them?*

My mind flashed back to the ball. The way each encounter was alike yet slightly different. Each touch familiar, yet strange. My heart pounded as it began to sink in.

I reached for my wine, gulping it down in one sip. My fingers trembled around the stem of the glass. "I wasn't myself last night... It can't be this way. No. I'll take my leave first thing in the morning."

Ramsay snickered. "We can't let you do that, Princess. The games have only just begun."

I struggled for breath, dizzy. "I am the future queen of Cinder Falls. You cannot keep me here as your prisoner."

"But if you leave, what will you go back to, Tallulah?" Bronte asked. "A boring life at Court with some idiot your parents select for you? Are you willing to spend night after night getting railed by his wrinkled cock just so you can produce his boring Fae children?"

My mouth dropped open. "Excuse me, sir, but that is quite inappropriate," I snapped.

Shadow yanked me closer to him. His green eyes were

almost black. "I know what you really want, Princess. We all do. You want to be our dirty little whore."

I sucked in a sharp breath, my nipples pebbling.

Shadow chuckled. "I remember how you loved when I called you that last night."

"Think long and hard about it, Princess," Ramsay murmured. "Sleep on it. By morning, if you want to leave, your horse will be out front waiting to take you away. But just know that if you walk out that door, you will never see us again."

"No, she must stay," Bronte cried out, slapping his hand on the table.

I flinched back.

Shadow's lips turned up into a deviant smirk. "Don't worry, brother. I have no doubt what her decision will be."

As tiny beads of moisture began to pool between my legs, I couldn't help but wonder if they were right. Did I want this? To be defiled by all three of them?

I pushed away from the table and backed up. "I-I need some rest. Thank you for dinner."

My body was betraying me, urging me to become enslaved to this desire. It was improper and indecent. I may have had my fun at the ball last night, but that was when I thought it was one man. Now that three of them stood before me, the weight of it hit me. This was too much.

"Who's ready for dessert? I made cherry cream pie," Lady George cooed as she sauntered back in, breaking the tension.

Shadow glared at me, taunting me with his ever-present smirk. "I believe the princess will be taking her cream in her room tonight. Isn't that right, Tallulah?"

Ramsay and Bronte both stifled a laugh.

Bastards.

I didn't need a mirror to see that my cheeks were bright red. The heat was crawling up my neck like a snake. But it wasn't shame. No. I was fucking pissed. How dare they?

I snatched a piece of pie off the table and dipped my finger into it. "Yes, that's right. Somehow it always tastes better when I'm alone." I shot Shadow a look of defiance as I sucked the cream off my finger.

"*Liar,*" he muttered under his breath.

Pretending to not hear my comment, Lady George hummed to herself as she dished out the rest of the pie.

Ramsay grumbled as he shoveled a huge bite into his mouth. And Bronte white-knuckled his fork like he was about to have another outburst. My courage was quickly returning at the sight of all three of them pouting.

My grin widened as I locked eyes with Shadow. "Goodnight, my Lords. Sweet dreams."

I had enjoyed messing with them, but a wash of nerves fluttered my belly as I crept down the dark hall to my room. I was in a strange manor, alone, with three volatile and feral Fae men. Fae men who had each already made me come undone at their hands. There was no light in this house. Their magic was dark and twisted.

But it was also seductive.

As I closed the door behind me, I didn't bother to lock it. This was their house, and they would find a way in if they wanted to. The thought sent a spasm straight to my nub.

They were all three right. I didn't want to live a boring

life, I wanted my freedom more than anything, and I would do just about anything to get it.

But if I gave in… what would they take in return?

I snapped my fingers and a shimmery light sparkled around me. My blue dress transformed into a thin white nightgown made of soft cotton. It felt smooth against my heated flesh.

And as I climbed into the enormous four-poster bed, a little rush of excitement shot through me, tempting me to stay and play their games.

CHAPTER 6

A cool draft swept over my skin. My eyes fluttered open. *How long had I been asleep for?* The room was dark except for the glow of embers, smoldering in the hearth.

A figure moved forward. "Want me to read you a bedtime story, Princess?"

My breath hitched. "Who's there?" I panicked.

He stood at the end of the bed, peering down at me with those electric green eyes. "The one you've been waiting for to set you free."

Underneath the sweet and polite façade, I was starting to realize that Bronte might be the most unhinged out of the three of them.

We reached for the covers at the same time. But he was

too quick. In seconds the top bedding was on the floor, and I laid there shivering. Vulnerable. Exposed with just a thin see-through nightgown.

"What are you doing?"

Bronte climbed onto the bed and placed one knee between my thighs. His lips curled into a half-smirk, half-snarl. *Feral.* "Whatever I want."

He inched his knee farther up, pushing my nightgown up around my waist, forcing me to spread my legs wider to accommodate his muscular frame. "You never finished your dessert, Princess. I didn't want you to go to bed *hungry.*"

A tremor rippled through my entire body. "*Bronte...*"

He slid his hands up my thighs and pressed them back against the bed. "Yes, Tulip. Say my name. Scream it loud while I'm destroying that sweet cunt of yours."

Oh, fuck.

Sweat pooled down my chest, trickling between my breasts. My swollen nipples threatened to poke two holes in the fabric of my nightgown. Before last night, no one had ever touched me before. And now I craved it. *Needed it.* But it was indecent.

"You think you can just come in here and have your way with me? This is not courtship, my Lord," I rasped.

Bronte ran his fingertips across the edges of my panties. "You are far away from the palace, Princess... There are no courts or formalities here."

I gasped as he pulled my panties to the side. The cool air hitting my scorching-hot flesh sent another tremble to my tender nub.

"You are so fucking wet for me. Tell me, Tulip, have you ever had a thick cock inside of that cunt of yours? Hmm?"

I shook my head, panting. "No," I whispered."

Bronte chuckled. "I didn't think so." He dragged one finger down the side of my pussy, and I almost came right there.

Goose pimples covered my flesh as he continued to trace slow circular movements around my nub. "Relax… you're not ready for my cock just yet. But I will enter that tight cunt in other ways."

I was near hyperventilation. The light as a feather strokes he was making to my aching pussy was pulling me into a state of delirium. I needed release so fucking bad.

While I was distracted, he grabbed my left wrist, pinned it over my head, and wound a rope around it, tying it tight to the bedpost. My heart raced. *Oh, gods.* He must have brought in the restraints while I was sleeping.

Bronte breathed heavy as he did the same to my other wrist. "When you give up control, the release is so much sweeter… Would you like that?"

My heart hammered. "*You're giving me a choice?*"

He caressed his palm against my aching nipple, and I could not stop myself from arching up toward it. "Princess, you made your choice the second you walked into this house. I'm just trying to give your brain a minute to catch up to your body. But if you insist, I will untie you right now."

I glanced up at my wrists, then back at him. "*No.*"

Bronte stilled. "No, what?"

"No… *don't stop,*" I pleaded.

He flashed a wicked grin. "That's my good little whore." He

pulled at my restraints, reaffirming that I was bound tight with no chance of escape. "Now I get to break you in."

Without warning, Bronte yanked my panties down and off. He held them to his face and inhaled, his lips quivering. I watched him, trembling, as he dragged the tip of his tongue across the crotch. "*So sticky*... like cherry cream pie."

A whimper escaped me. What was happening to me right now? This was dirty and yet I wanted more. So much more.

I drew in a sharp breath as he slowly ripped my nightgown in two and pulled it back from my body. I was completely exposed now.

His eyes burned into mine as he began removing his own clothes with careful precision. He grinned as my eyes widened at the sight of his chiseled chest, the way his muscles carved in and out as if they were created by the gods themselves. His smooth cock stood erect, so big I wondered how it would possibly fit inside me. But oh, how I wanted to feel him bruise me with it.

"You will have my cock soon enough, Princess. But tonight, I get to play with you."

Bronte reached across me and grabbed my uneaten plate of cherry cream pie. He scooped some out and smeared it down my wet slit. I twitched as the sticky cream oozed down between my folds. "Oh, *fuck*. Bronte...What are... you doing?" I had never felt so aroused in my entire life.

He bent down, his lips hovering over my soiled pussy. "Having my pie and eating it too."

I gasped as he licked me from taint to nub. He pressed

his tongue firm against me, collecting the cream in his mouth, moaning as he lapped at it. I bucked as he pushed his tongue inside me. He pressed my thighs back wider, his fingers digging into my hips. I couldn't breathe.

"*Fuck,*" I cried out, clenching as stars blurred my vision.

He pressed on my throbbing nub. "Relax… Open up for me, Tulip."

I struggled to reclaim my own body. But it was no use. He was in control. And I wanted to surrender.

I unclenched and released another quivering breath. A fresh pool of moisture trickled out of my pussy, dripping down my slit.

Bronte moved up beside me and inserted one finger inside. "That's it. Yes… just like that, Tulip."

I moaned as he slid his finger in and out slowly.

"I want to feel you stretch for me," he breathed.

Bronte added another finger as he slid back in.

I arched back, writhing on the soiled sheets. I needed to touch him. Needed to touch myself. But the more I struggled, the more the ropes dug into my wrists. "Bronte… please."

He pushed his fingers deeper inside. "Fuck… you are doing so good. Taking it like the good little slut you are. I can't wait to bury my cock inside this dirty fucking cunt."

A wave of euphoria climbed inside me. I was so close to the edge. So close to exploding all over him. I rolled my hips as he continued to thrust in and out.

"More," I begged.

Bronte chuckled as he reached over with his other hand

and pulled the folds of my pussy back. "Grind against my hand, Tulip. *Show* me you want more."

I cried out in frustration, in need, as I thrusted my pussy into his hand, his two fingers still deep inside me. I lifted my hips as he teased me, pulling his hand away and then back. "Bronte, I need to…"

"I know what you fucking need, Tulip."

As I rose up again he shoved a third finger inside me. I screamed as he pressed them hard against a spot I didn't even know I had. I was done for.

Pressure built inside and spread out, tingling every inch of my flesh as my orgasm took hold of me. My vision went black as I released my juices into his grip.

He licked my nipples as I came undone. "Yes, Tulip. Let it all out. Give in to what you want."

I panted as the tingling spread to my nipples, my belly, and my ass. Every nerve in my body was on fire. Every touch, enough to send me into another orgasm.

Bronte licked his fingers clean. "See… I told you I could break her."

Wait. What?

I looked up to see two figures at the foot of the bed.

Shame and embarrassment suddenly filled me. Then rage. "You were watching us?"

Ramsay and Shadow both glared down at me, their eyes full of lust and hunger.

I flinched as Bronte dragged his finger across my swollen clit. "That's not all they'll do, Princess. You're *our* little whore. And each one of us will break you."

Panic washed over me. I was tied up and naked while three feral deviant men surrounded me. "Get out, all three of you. Or I will scream for Lady George."

Ramsay snickered. "Lady George isn't here, Princess. She lives in the guest house down the road. It's just us now."

What? Oh, fuck. Now I was in trouble. But was I mad, terrified, or even more turned on?

"Untie her, Bronte," Shadow's raspy voice cut in. "Let the princess get some rest. She's going to need it."

Bronte pouted as he rubbed one of my nipples between his fingers. "But I want to keep playing with her."

Oh gods. I was wet again. And now that I knew I had an audience, heat pooled like a fire in my belly.

Ramsay walked to the other side of the bed and wrapped his hand around my bound wrist. "Why don't we ask the princess, brother? Tulip, do you want to play another game?"

Shadow shook his head. "Not tonight."

Bronte looked down at me. "Tell us what *you* want, Princess."

I was shaking. The thought of what they would do to me made me clench. "What… what kind of game?" I asked shyly.

Shadow growled. "Do as you please. I'm done for tonight." He stalked to the door and slammed it behind him.

Ramsay hissed. "Don't mind him, Princess. He's just in one of his moods."

Bronte caressed my thigh, tickling my flesh with his fingertips. "Perhaps he's right. We don't want to wear her out too quickly."

Ramsay joined us on the bed, nestling in next to me. "Except that filthy cunt of hers is dripping wet again…"

The heat from their bodies was driving me wild. I was overstimulated and yet somehow I wasn't ready for it to end tonight. "Just one more game," I whispered.

Ramsay unbuckled his leather belt and slid it off. "Stretch her open for me."

Oh, fuck.

Bronte slid his fingers down my slit and then peeled my folds back. I flinched as Ramsay pressed his belt against my sopping wet pussy. "I want to smell you on this later."

He pulled it taut between his fists and began rubbing it back and forth against me while Bronte held me wide open. A deep moan escaped me as the rough leather slid up and down my slit, every weathered groove stretching the delicate tissues of my flesh.

While Bronte was soft and gentle, Ramsay was far from it. He was rough and brutal, and it awakened something so feral in me, I thought I might rip through my restraints.

"I knew you had a beast inside you, Princess. Just waiting to come out," Ramsay cooed in my ear.

I couldn't hold back any longer. A deep guttural cry poured out of me as I claimed my peak.

Bronte stroked my belly. "Yes, Tulip. Let it consume you." He released my bindings and my wrists fell down like dead weights.

Ramsay gathered me in his arms. "I knew you were one of us from the second I saw you. You love our little games, don't you?"

My mouth was dry, and I could barely open my eyes. I whimpered into his neck as Bronte massaged my back. "Time to rest now, Tulip."

"Yes," Ramsay added. "Tomorrow we will play another game."

CHAPTER 7

Food tasted better this morning. Sweeter. Saltier. Alive on my tongue. Lady George hummed as she buzzed around the breakfast table, filling our plates with sugary confections.

"Your wrists appear to be healed, Princess," Shadow grumbled. "What a shame."

I rubbed at my skin. I may have healed myself on the surface, but the memory of the ropes burning into my skin was still fresh.

"What happened to your wrists, child?" Lady George asked.

Ramsay snickered. "That will be all, Lady. Please return to your quarters until supper."

Lady George opened her mouth to protest but then seemed to remember her place. The precious lords she raised were no longer children, and they made no secret of who was in charge now.

She gave them each a slight bow before leaving. "As you wish."

I was alone and at their mercy. Again.

Ramsay turned his ire on me. "Never again, Princess."

I nearly choked on a piece of glazed bread. "Excuse me?"

"You will wear our marks on you like the good little whore you are," Ramsay hissed.

I should have been offended and repulsed. But his possessiveness stirred something wild in me. "So you want to stifle my magic such as the queen does? And here I thought you were different."

Shadow smiled but it didn't reach his eyes. "That's not what he said. You may use your magic as you see fit. *Except* when it comes to us."

He really was a bastard.

"When you heal our marks, it's like you are ashamed of us," Bronte chimed in.

Heat rose to my cheeks. "I don't know what to feel right now…"

My appetite had suddenly left me. I was in over my head. These three wicked and infuriating men were pushing my limits. Well, I could push back. "You want to brand me like a horse, do you? Like I'm a piece of property. Shall I sleep in the stables too?"

Shadow leapt out of his chair and rushed toward me. He wrapped his hand around my throat, tipping my chair back so I had to look up at him as he squeezed. "That can be arranged. In case I decide to ride you like a fucking horse."

As I panted for air, moisture pooled between my thighs.

"Easy, brother. She's not ready for you yet," Ramsay called out.

Shadow loosened his grip but didn't let go. "She was plenty ready when I had her spread against the palace window."

I clenched as I remembered. *It was him.* His fingers were inside me right before midnight. It was Shadow who dropped the cuff link at the ball. I glared back at him defiantly. "Fuck you," I rasped.

He dug his fingers into the side of my neck and whispered, "Oh, you will, Princess. One of these nights you will fuck me until I give you permission to stop."

I flew forward as he released me, catching myself with the edge of the table. On instinct, magic rustled in my fingers as I reached for my throat.

"Ah, ah, ah, Princess," Shadow chided. "Don't even think about it."

I stilled my hands to my side as heat rushed to my cheeks. He was trying to humiliate me now. "I am the future Queen of Cinder Falls. Show a little respect."

Shadow slammed his fists on the table, causing all of us to jump. "And we are the lords of this manor. You will get respect when you earn it."

More than ever now I wished I possessed dark Fae magic just so I could bring him to his knees. I brought my hands back up to my throat, the magic tingling through my fingertips, aching to soothe my raw flesh.

"Stop. Right. Now," Shadow ordered.

A smirk brushed across my lips. "And if I don't?"

He clenched his fists. "Then I will bend you over my knee and mark that lily-white ass of yours until you do."

A little tingle stirred between my thighs. But I wouldn't give in. "And I'll just heal those marks too."

Shadow stood up so fast; his chair flew backward. He started toward me, but Ramsay held him in place.

Bronte let out a deep sigh. "Can the two of you hate fuck each other's eyes out on your own time? I'm trying to enjoy my breakfast."

I may have pushed too far. I lowered my hands to the table and continued eating. "Fine by me."

Shadow grunted as he sat back down, but he kept his murderous gaze locked on me. "Be careful what you wish for, Princess. You might not like the games I play."

A trickle of fear gripped me. This man was different. He didn't seem to even like me. And yet I knew by the way his cock tented his pants that I was getting under his skin. I was both terrified and intrigued by him.

The truth was I didn't want to heal my neck. No. I wanted his mark on me. His touch was like fire and despite my better judgement... I knew in that moment that I was going to let him burn me.

I spent the rest of the day wandering the grounds. While the house itself was dark and ominous, there was a beautiful bright courtyard and garden outside. A large stone fountain shaped in the form of three snakes, sat in the center. It was a bit creepy but the colorful flowers surrounding it seemed to make it more inviting.

I nestled myself into the grass, enjoying the way the soft blades felt against my bare shoulders. I had opted to dress a bit more modestly today—a strapless sundress that hung all the way down past my knees. I kicked off my shoes and dug my bare feet into the dirt. I would have never been able to lounge like this at the palace. The queen was always so concerned with appearances. And gods forbid I actually got to enjoy a moment of pleasure under her watch.

I closed my eyes, intoxicated by the warm sun on my face. It was peaceful here despite the untethered lords of Frost Manor. A part of me wished I didn't have to go back to the palace.

The sound of boots crunching over dry leaves broke my reverie. I opened my eyes to see Ramsay towering over me, blocking the sun. "Hello, Tulip. That was quite the display you put on this morning."

I sighed. "Come to taunt me some more, Ramsay?"

He kneeled in front of me and grabbed my chin, pinching it between his smooth fingers. "You shouldn't aggravate Shadow like that. He is… merciless."

I was being pulled into their darkness like a magnet, caught in their seductive web. It was addictive. "Why is he so angry all the time?"

"He has been that way since we were kids. That is just who he is. Perhaps it's because he's a bastard," Ramsay snickered.

"And what about you? Why are you such a pain in the ass?" I quipped.

Ramsay hissed and pushed me back, pinning my arms above my head. My heart pounded as he dragged his tongue up my jaw. "Pain… pleasure… it's one and the same. You know that better than anyone, Princess."

My breath hitched as he placed soft kisses down my neck. "What is that saying, Tulip? Hmm? Don't throw stones at glass houses… We've all heard the whisperings of the palace staff. How your stepmother despises you. How she blames you for your baby brother's accident… You may wear a crown upon your head, but you are no different from any of us."

A boiling rage stirred inside me. My cheeks flamed as I wriggled out of his grasp and shoved him back. "You know nothing about my life. *Nothing.*"

Ramsay chuckled as he boxed me in again. A dark mischievousness flickered in his piercing green eyes. "Own that pain, Tallulah. *Claim it.* And then use it to destroy all those who hurt you. They will never see it coming."

My entire life, I had been at the mercy of others. My father, my stepmother, my own guards. Even now, I was making choices based on what my family expected. I'd been acting desperate, reckless, and foolish. Ramsay was right. I was the future Queen of Cinder Falls. I needed to start acting like it.

An ache stirred in me. As I gazed at him, his beauty took my breath away. I wanted him. I wanted all three of them. His eyes widened as I grabbed his face and pulled it toward mine. We both gasped as our lips met. He shoved his tongue deep into my mouth as I kissed him hard. Our breaths tangled.

He tasted like winter—like night—like dark skies, silvery moons, and starlight. His lips full and soft, bruising mine in a frenzied rush to consume. His tongue was my anchor, commanding me to get lost inside his darkness. I wanted so much from him. I needed it.

I laid back against the grass, pulling him with me. "Play with me, Ramsay."

"Oh, you wicked little thing. So naughty. Do as I tell you, or I'll stop," he growled.

I nodded, breathless, my clit tingling in anticipation. "Please..."

He pulled the hem of my dress up around my waist. "Spread your legs nice and wide for me."

The sun warmed my exposed flesh as I obeyed his command. A lightness spread throughout my body. A dizziness. He licked his lips, his gaze fixated on my moistened panties. I rolled my hips, urging him to keep going.

His breath hitched as he pulled my panties to the side. "You *intoxicate* me, Princess. I'm going to make you cum slow and hard."

Oh, fuck. I was already throbbing with need.

Ramsay plucked out a blade of grass and dragged the tip of it up my slit. "And I'm going to do it without even touching you."

He drew circles around my clit. The light tickle sent my body into shivers. I would never have imagined that this tiny little blade of grass, under his command, could bring me to near convulsions.

Without warning, he ripped my panties down the center

and tore them away from me. "That's better. Keep your legs nice and spread for me, Tulip."

He smirked as he plucked out another blade and began tracing it over my swollen nub while he continued to stroke the other one up and down my wet slit.

"Fuck…" I rasped. My legs trembled at the stimulation. Little bursts of white light clouded my vision. I jerked my hips as the pressure built.

Ramsay licked his lips. "You're such a good little whore for me, Tulip. Fuck, I'm going to get you so dirty."

The tips of the blades felt like needles and feathers at the same time, poking and caressing my entrance. The lips of my pussy pulsed, ached, as the vibrations moved deeper inside me to my core. Spreading my legs as far as they would go, he let out a growl. "Yes, Tulip. Open up for me. Let me see every inch of you."

I cried out, arching my back, my shoulders pressing hard into the ground. My breaths became quivers as I dug my nails into the dirt, desperate for release. He quickened his pace, circling my nub with one while sliding the other blade deeper inside.

"Ramsay. Fuck. I'm…" A guttural scream escaped from deep inside my chest as the throbbing seized my swollen clit and spread inside me. The tender flesh of my pussy twitched as my cream spilled out.

He dug his fingers into my thighs, pressing them hard against the ground as I bucked and thrashed my hips, another orgasm taking hold of me. Our eyes locked, and I could see that it was taking every ounce of his willpower not to pounce on me.

"Please, Ramsay... I need you inside me," I begged.

A soft moan rumbled out of him. Sweat beaded his temples. "But you've been a bad girl, Tulip. So defiant. Only good little whores get what they want."

I cried out in frustration. I had just cum twice in a row, but I wanted more. "What more do you want from me?"

He flashed a devilish grin. "*Everything*. You need to stop holding back. Own what you want. Take it from each one of us. If you don't fully let go, Princess, this fleeting pleasure will never be enough."

I shuddered as he released my legs and stalked off. I laid there panting in the grass, shaking, and more awake than I'd ever been.

CHAPTER 8

I stumbled into the house, a fumbling mess. With grass stains on my dress and dirt caked into my nails and feet, I felt feral.

Bronte cornered me in the hallway. "You're tracking mud all through the house, Princess."

"It's Ramsay's fault," I snapped.

"Let's get you cleaned up then." He pulled a leaf from my disheveled hair. "There's a hot soapy bath waiting for you in my room."

Their eyes were always on me, watching every move I made. "You saw us in the garden, didn't you?"

Bronte snaked an arm around my waist, pulling me with him as he walked. "Tallulah, darling, when are you going to realize that you belong to all of us? There are no secrets in this house."

I swallowed hard as we approached his room. They didn't want me to choose one of them. They wanted me to give myself to *all* of them. I had never heard of such a thing before. But the longer I stayed in this house, the more rational it seemed. The idea of being shared by them thrilled me in ways I'd never imagined.

Bronte guided me inside and shut the door behind us. His room had all the comforts of mine—a plush four-poster bed, a large stone fireplace, and a magnificent porcelain tub. Except his was in the center of the room as if it were the focal point.

The steam sizzled off the top, carrying scents of roses and gardenia into the air. My heart skipped a beat. I couldn't wait to sink deep down into it.

My breath quickened at the feel of Bronte's fingers unzipping me. My dress fell to the floor. And since Ramsay had already torn my panties to shreds, I stood there completely naked and covered in filth.

He walked around to my front, his gaze traveling over every inch of me. "Get in the bath, Tulip. If you're good, I'll reward you."

My belly fluttered. The memory of his mouth on my pussy made me clench. His soft lips and fingers exploring every crevice. I sucked in a sharp breath and stepped into the soapy water. My muscles instantly relaxed as I sank down.

Bronte pulled up a chair next to me. "Hand me that

sponge." He rolled up his sleeves and dipped it in the water. "I'm going to take care of you, Tulip."

I closed my eyes and leaned back as he dragged the sponge across my chest. He lightly scrubbed at my skin. "Arch your back for me. Let me clean every inch of you."

The cool air hit my nipples, pebbling them as I lifted my chest out of the water. I drew in a sharp breath as Bronte rung out the sponge over my breasts.

"That's it. Look at those pretty pink nipples. So hard for me." He massaged the sponge between my breasts, circling my nipples with an agonizing slowness. I gripped the sides of the tub, ravenous for more.

He dragged the soapy sponge down my belly, stilling it right above my clit. "Do you want me to clean that filthy pussy of yours, Tulip?"

I whimpered and twisted in the water, my heart beating so loud I thought it might fly out of my chest. "Yes, *please*, Bronte."

He licked his lips. "Mmm. That's a good little whore."

I gasped as he wiped the sponge up and down my slit. The ridges of the sponge rubbed against my throbbing folds. I moaned and spread my legs, my knees hitting the sides of the tub with a bang.

"Oh, you want me to go deeper, do you? Gods I love the way you behave for me." He pushed the sponge firm against my nub before dragging it back down my slit and inserting the tip inside.

I bucked as he twisted it back and forth in a circular motion. "*Oh, fuck*," I cried out.

"I'm going to get you so fucking clean, Tallulah. Relax… you're so tight. Let me in."

Every nerve in my body was on fire, but all I could focus on was the pressure building in my walls. I released a shuddering breath as Bronte pushed the sponge deeper inside of me. It expanded inside my pussy. Every ridge of it pressing into me and pushing me closer to the edge. I rocked into it, letting him fuck me with it.

His free hand slid down my back. "Take a deep breath for me, Tulip."

I felt his fingers on the base of my spine while he twisted the sponge deeper inside me. I was panting now. "Yes… don't stop."

He chuckled and slid a finger down the slit of my ass. "You are doing so good. Are you going to let me all the way in?"

Oh, fuck. As I realized what he was going to do next, I clenched around him on instinct.

"Relax, Tulip. Surrender to it." He inserted his finger between my ass cheeks and pushed at my entrance.

Fuck. It ached. Throbbed. He rubbed back and forth gently, and it sent a pulse straight to my clit. I unclenched my muscles and exhaled the breath I was holding. "*Fuck,*" I whispered.

And that was all he needed.

With one quick thrust, he sank his finger inside my ass. I jerked my hips. "Bronte… fuck why does that feel so good?"

"That's my good little whore. Taking it so deep. I'm going to milk every drop of cream from you."

He pumped his finger in and out while still twisting the sponge inside my pussy. It was enough to make me pass out from pleasure. The water splashed over the sides of the tub as I bucked back and forth between the palms of his hands.

"Oh, shit," I panted.

White stars clouded my vision as he guided me toward my peak. His fingers clawed at my insides, pressing on all my pleasure spots. He was literally dragging it out of me. I let out a loud moan as I writhed against his hands.

"Yes, Tulip. Fuck, yes," he praised.

Bronte lifted me out of the tub and carried me over to the bed. He laid me down and stood by my feet. "Now I want to watch."

My legs shook as my orgasm still rippled through me. "Watch what?"

He smiled like the devil. "I want to watch you touch yourself."

My pussy still throbbed. Still so fucking wet.

I inched my hand down, settling it between my legs. "Tell me what you want me to do..."

He drew in a deep raspy breath. "Open up nice and wide for me."

I spread my legs far apart, pulling my heels in toward my ass.

"Yeah, just like that. Now, I want you to slide your finger up and down that glistening cunt. Right down the fucking middle."

I arched my hips as a new sensation took hold of me. A feeling of power even though I was under his command.

"Pinch your right nipple hard for me. Don't stop until I tell you to."

I moaned and squeezed my swollen nipple, a shock of pleasure rippling through me.

His eyes turned feral. "I could watch you play with yourself all night."

I continued to slide my finger up and down my sopping wet slit.

"Push it in, Princess."

I hesitated. "Inside?"

He climbed onto the bed next to me and nibbled on my earlobe. "Yes. Put your finger deep inside your cunt. I want to watch you fuck yourself."

As I pushed the tip of my finger inside, a wave of heat flooded my belly. "Oh, fuck."

He pressed in closer. "Mmm… fuck. How does that feel?"

"So good…."

"Yeah. You look like a queen right now. Owning your own pleasure."

He stroked my thigh as I fingered myself. The act of him watching me aroused me even more.

"Bring your other hand down here, Tallulah. Spread yourself apart."

"Like this?" I panted. I peeled back the folds of my flesh with two fingers.

"Yes… just like that. Go nice and slow. In and out. I want you to beg me to let you cum."

As I slid my finger in and out of my pussy, the door

creaked open. Ramsay and Shadow walked in, an air of carnal hunger surrounding them.

My gaze darted back and forth between the three of them. I should have leapt off the bed. Should have scrambled for my clothes. But being under his control felt too good. The idea of all three of them watching me, pushed me even closer to the edge. I couldn't stop.

Ramsay leaned against the bedpost while Shadow stayed at the foot of the bed.

Bronte kissed my neck. "You like putting on a show for us, don't you? Keep going just like that, nice and slow."

"One finger isn't enough. Add another," Shadow growled.

I looked at Bronte for permission.

"Do as he says, Tallulah. You belong to all of us."

My heart raced as I inserted another finger. "Ohhh…"

Ramsay pressed his fists into the mattress between my thighs, fixated on my sopping wet pussy. "*Own it*, Tallulah."

I let out a blood curdling cry as I stretched myself out around my fingers. I pumped faster. They watched me like animals zeroing in on their prey as I jerked back and forth on the bed, thrusting my hips up and down like a wild beast.

"Don't stop," Bronte rasped. He took one of my nipples in his mouth and sucked.

"Harder now, Tulip. *Deeper*." Ramsay pressed my thighs back as I pushed all the way in past my knuckles.

Bronte scraped his teeth against my throbbing nipple. "Be a good little whore and cum for us now."

His words triggered me. I circled my thumb around my

clit as another orgasm thrummed through me. "Gods... fuck," I yelled.

Hot cream coated my fingers as I thrusted. "*Fuck,*" I whispered.

Bronte grabbed my hand and brought it to his lips. "Let me taste my reward."

He put one of my cum-soaked fingers into his mouth and sucked, moaning as he slurped it off. Ramsay did the same, sucking my cream off the other finger. It was the most erotic thing I had ever experienced.

As Shadow approached, I held my hand out. Instead of taking it, he snarled and yanked my hips to the edge of the bed. Fear gripped me.

"I'll help myself to what I want," he snapped.

I whimpered as he bent down and dragged his tongue slowly up my slit, stilling at my clit. He puckered his lips around my nub and sucked so hard, another tremor shot through me. "Fuck. I'm coming again," I dug my fingers into his hair as he lapped at my freshly spilt juices.

Shadow licked away every trace. "You will not play me the way you do my brothers, Princess." He wiped his mouth with the back of his hand and stalked out.

"What did I do?" I asked, confused.

Ramsay cupped my cheek in his palm. "You are breaking him open, Tulip. I'd call that a win."

Why wasn't I satisfied with just Ramsay and Bronte's adoration? Why did I need Shadow to look at me the way they did too?

Bronte covered me with a blanket. "Sleep now, Tulip. Shadow will claim you when he's ready."

I rolled over and nestled myself into the sheets of Bronte's bed. As I replayed the whole night over again in my head, I shuddered the most when I thought of Shadow's brutal tongue lashing at my flesh. What Ramsay and Bronte didn't realize was that he claimed me the second our eyes locked at the ball.

And I claimed them.

Ramsay, Bronte… Shadow.

They were mine.

CHAPTER 9

The sound of blackbirds chirping outside my window coaxed me awake. I yawned and stretched inside the tangled sheets. My limbs were sore, my pussy raw from being stroked and licked. A tiny shiver swept up my back as I replayed last night's scene in my head.

Heat flooded my body, the sheets caressing my naked flesh as I writhed underneath them. Just the thought of the three of them drove me to the edge. I was becoming obsessed with their touch, their dirty words… their vulgarity.

And something new sparked in me. A rush of adrenaline mixed with a desperate desire to show them what they were doing to me. To make them see how fucking needy I was for them.

I bounced out of bed, pulled on my robe, and stepped out into the hallway. It was indecent but I didn't care. I crept past Bronte's empty room to another set of doors at the end of the hall. Two were locked. But the third one opened when I turned the knob.

With only one window streaming in the early dawn, the room was darker than mine. There was a modest queen-sized bed, a hearth, and a bookcase sat against the far wall. I tip-toed barefoot on the wood floor to explore more. The room was gigantic. I ran my hand across the velvet-tapestried wall as I walked.

"You lost, Princess?" Shadow's gruff voice cut through the dark like a knife.

My heart raced as I spun in his direction. Spotting him in the far corner of the room, my juices pooled. He was sitting on one of a set of two brown leather couches. Wearing only a robe himself, his legs were parted, the robe slightly open, revealing his perfectly chiseled abs and muscular thighs.

"I've been lost for a very long time," I murmured back as I inched closer to the sitting area.

He took a sip out of his steaming mug. "And now? Have you been found?"

The way he licked his lips sent tingles down my legs. "I believe so."

Shadow's eyes darkened. "What are you doing in here, Princess? An innocent little girl like you should know better than to go wandering around in the dark."

I slithered onto the other couch across from him, my courage growing. He terrified me but in the most delightful way. I loosened my robe and slightly parted my legs, mimicking his position. "The light has stifled me. But in the dark I feel free."

His lips curled into a snarl as he fixated on the knot in my robe. "Dirty things happen in the dark, Princess. Filthy shameful things that you can't undo. Is that what you want? To be my dirty little secret in the dark?"

My breath hitched. An ache began to form in my middle, pushing me to the edge of all things decent. Urging me to leave behind any sense of self-preservation or civility. I wanted him to give in to me. To trust me. I wanted him to see...

I untied my robe and pulled it back away from my body. "I'm not afraid of the dark. And I'm not afraid of you, Shadow. If you don't want to admit that you enjoyed having your fingers inside of me, then that's your cross to bear. You can pretend it was all a game, but I know the truth. I can see the hunger in your eyes. You want me just as bad as I want you."

He took another sip from his mug, glaring at me over the rim. "You may have Ramsay and Bronte wrapped around your little finger, but I can't be so easily seduced. Do whatever you want, Princess. It makes no difference to me."

His fingers gripped the mug as his throat bobbed. I smirked and ran my fingers down my thighs. "Then why are you still here?"

"I was here first," he rasped.

I shrugged. "True. Shall I leave then?" I slid my hands in between my thighs.

Shadow fixated on where my fingers would go next. "As I said, you can do whatever you want. I won't stop you."

He had his walls up for so long, he would do everything in his power to hold them up. But the cracks were showing. And I was gaining the upper hand. I smiled sweetly and arched my back.

"Do you like looking at me, Shadow?" I drew my hands up to my chest, circling my swollen nipples with my fingertips.

"It's amusing that you think you have some sort of control over me, Princess. It's nothing I haven't seen before."

Liar. A fresh sheen of sweat coated his brow.

I pinched my nipples hard between my fingers, throwing my head back as I let out a soft whimper. "*Fuck...* When I touch myself, Shadow, I imagine that it's your hands on me."

He snickered. "You are far too gentle to pretend you're me."

I chuckled as I met his feral gaze. "That's because slow and gentle is agonizing for you."

The heat in my body increased, spreading to every deviant part of me. I stretched my legs wider as I slid a finger down my wet slit. My hips bucked at the contact. The act of touching myself as he watched unhinged me. I needed to control myself. Drawing this out as long as possible would drive him mad. And I relished the thought.

Shadow shifted in his seat, trying to cover his erection with his robe, and opened a drawer from the table next to the couch. "I'll play your little game, Princess. But I'm going to play it my way. If you really want to show me what a dirty little girl you are, then let's see what you can do with this." He tossed me a glass wand and returned to his seat.

Without hesitating I wrapped my lips around it, coating it with my saliva. I sucked on it, twisting it around in my mouth.

His lips parted as he released a quivering breath.

I dragged the tip of the wand between my breasts, down my belly, and rested it against my aching nub.

"Mmm," I moaned as I rubbed it against me.

I scooted down, opening my legs wider. "Do you want to see me pleasure myself, Shadow?"

He let out a growl.

"I think you do." I inserted the tip of the wand into my pussy. "Uhhh, fuck." Arching my hips, I slid it further inside. My insides clenched around it. It was cool and slick. I stretched the folds of my pussy open with my other hand and pushed the wand further inside.

"Fuck," he breathed as he leaned forward, watching my every move. "You're so fucking tight."

"Y-yes," I panted. A wave of tingles erupted inside of me, my blood rushing to my clit as I inched it further in. A mixture of pleasure and pain as I stretched around it. I fingered my clit as the pressure in my belly grew. I cried out as the whole of the wand finally nestled deep inside.

I locked my gaze to his as I pulled the wand out slowly and then slid it back in, rocking back and forth against it.

Shadow licked his lips as he watched. "It is agonizing…"

Sweat dripped down my body as I ground against the

wand, every nerve on fire. But I wasn't done toying with him yet. "Maybe I don't need you after all," I cooed.

His nostrils flared as he let out a deep growl. In a flash, he was on his feet. He towered over me as I continued to slide the wand in and out of my swollen pussy. With his robe hanging open, he couldn't hide how hard he was for me now.

"You think you can do a better job of making yourself cum than I can, Princess?" He sat down next to me.

I grabbed his hand and guided it over to the wand. "Prove me wrong, Shadow."

He sniffed my neck, tracing his lips up my jaw until he got to my ear. "I'm not falling for your tricks, Princess. You are the only one who has something you feel you need to prove. You and I both know how hard I can make you cum."

Fuck. I wanted him to touch me so bad. But he was as stubborn as an ox. He wanted more. And so I would give it to him.

I moved to the coffee table and laid out across it, draping my legs over the sides. At this angle, I could push the wand in deeper. I thrusted harder, faster, my wrist and arm aching from the force. "Isn't this enough for you?" I breathed. "Tell me what more can I give."

Shadow walked over to a chest against the far wall. He opened it and reached inside, pulling out a black silk scarf, and a dagger with a pearl encrusted hilt.

My heart raced as he stood over me. "What is all that for?"

His eyes blazed with hunger. "For getting you nice and dirty. Now keep that wand deep inside your cunt for me."

I stilled my hand as he brought my other one to rest on the wand. He smirked as he wrapped the silk scarf around my wrists and tied them tight together. "Continue."

More juices flowed out as I worked the wand in and out of my pussy, my wrists bound. The scarf dug into my flesh, burning me as I thrusted. A dozen different sensations hit me all at once as I felt my climax building. "Oh, gods… I'm going to cum soon."

Shadow dragged the tip of the dagger down my thigh. "Not yet, Princess. Not until I've tasted the arousal in your blood."

What the hell? I started to sit up, fear taking hold of me.

"Too late to stop now, Princess. I'm going to take what I want now." He shoved me back down against the coffee table. "Relax… embrace the darkness." He covered my hands with his and pushed down. I gasped as the wand slid back in. He pushed and pulled my hands, in and out. "Just like that. Don't stop."

I nodded and took a deep breath. I couldn't help but be turned on despite my fear. He was my trigger. My monster.

Shadow knelt down beside me. "This will sting for a minute."

I flinched as he nicked my flesh with the dagger. Ruby red blood trickled out. It stung and throbbed. But as soon as his tongue and lips covered it, a warm dizzying sensation took over. It was fucking ecstasy. I cried out and clenched around the wand.

"Fuck you taste good, Princess." He sucked my wound.

Without even thinking, my magic began to heal it. "Did you like that?" He asked.

I didn't know. Did I? I didn't hate it. "Again," I commanded.

He dug the tip of the blade in a little deeper this time and I bucked the second his tongue seared my flesh. He moaned as he drank my blood.

As my magic began to heal the fresh wound, a tremor deep inside my pussy seized me. "Oh fuck," I screamed.

He squeezed my hands, forcing the wand deeper inside as I exploded all over it. I thrusted up as he pressed me down, grinding against it, desperate to claim every inch of it. Stretching out my orgasm for as long as the gods would let me.

I whimpered as Shadow pulled it out of me slowly, my muscles twitching as it left my body.

He grabbed me by the hair and sat me upright. "Now be a good little whore and clean my wand for me."

I stared at the wand, my juices smeared all over it, realizing what he wanted me to do. He was right. This was far dirtier than anything I had planned.

He tightened his grip, pulling my strands hard. "Open your fucking mouth and clean up your mess."

With my wrists still bound I took the wand from his hands and put it in my mouth. The taste of my own cum on my tongue sparked something carnal in me. I moaned as I sucked, twisting the wand inside my mouth, desperate to consume every drop.

"I knew you liked dirty things. Don't stop until I say so."

My eyes glazed with tears as he shoved the wand deeper in, until it hit the back of my throat.

"Don't cry, Princess. This is nothing. I'll be far more brutal when you're sucking *my* cock," he rasped.

I gasped for air when he finally removed the wand from my mouth. This whole morning had not been what I expected. I couldn't explain how or why, but my body was in a constant state of arousal in this house.

I started to get up and he shoved me back down again. "You're not finished cleaning yourself, Princess."

Confusion came over me. "What do you mean?"

He dragged the tip of the dagger down my thigh, light enough to not break skin but still firm enough to scratch. *"Your pussy is still full of cream,"* he growled. "I want to see you wipe up every drop."

Oh, gods. I was going to cum again. Maybe that's what he wanted. Just one of his sick and twisted games to keep me in a perpetual state of wanting and agony.

I leaned back and spread my legs. "I can't promise I won't make a mess again."

Shadow wrapped his hand around my throat and squeezed. "I'm not letting you off this table until that dirty pussy of yours is clean."

I dipped two fingers inside my folds and coated them in my juices. As I brought my fingers to my mouth and sucked, Shadow shivered. His grip tightened on my throat. "That's it. Just like that. Again."

I could barely breathe with his hand around my throat,

and it was sending tingles to my nub again. I sucked my fingers over and over again, each time making me wetter.

Shadow slid behind me, so I was in his lap. He squeezed my throat harder. "Don't play with me, Princess. Push those fingers deep inside. *Get them nice and wet.*"

As I did as he commanded, my hips bucked, the pressure in my clit building again. His cock stiffened against my back. "I know you want to fuck yourself against me, Princess."

A deep moan billowed out of me. "You tricked me."

"It is you who came here with tricks. Try me again and I will lock you in the cellar and torture you until you obey me. Now show me what a good fucking whore you are and make that pussy cum for me again."

Oh, gods. I was so turned on. So fucking swept away in this naughty game we were playing. "You win," I breathed.

I pumped my fingers in and out, writhing my hips against him as I fucked myself. The harder I pounded, the harder his erection grew against my back, and the tighter his grip was around my throat.

I threw my head back, banging it on his shoulder as another orgasm seized me. I dug my fingers in deeper, swirling them around my folds as I came on them. In my attempt to drag it out, a second wave gripped me.

"*Yes, Princess. Destroy yourself for me.*"

I slumped back in his arms, overwhelmed, as tears streamed down my cheeks. Every move he made was calculated, cunning, and cold.

"And when will *you* destroy yourself *for me*, Shadow?"

He's claimed me again and again, but I still couldn't break down his walls.

He slid away from me. "There are parts of me that need to stay locked up tight. Believe me, Princess. You would not like what you see."

I pulled my robe to my chest, suddenly feeling more vulnerable than ever. "Maybe I'd surprise you. Maybe… I'd love it."

Shadow shook his head. "No one loves monsters. Not even broken little Fae princesses with daddy issues."

My mouth gaped open. "I am none of those things." Heat rushed to my cheeks. What the fuck did he know about me, anyway?

He arched an eyebrow. "Aren't you, though? If you were whole, you'd have never left the palace. Never would have let three deviants defile you like a common whore."

Shame quickly turned to rage. "You really are a fucking bastard."

CHAPTER 10

I avoided Shadow's gaze as I sauntered into the dining room. Ramsay and Bronte eyed me cautiously as I took the farthest seat away from all three of them. They must have known something happened between me and Shadow. Hell, they were probably listening at the door.

Lady George hummed around the table as usual. "Good morning, Tallulah! I trust that you slept well?"

I forced a smile. "Yes, it was the waking up that was a bit rough."

Ramsay and Bronte both stifled a laugh.

"Something funny?" I asked. Heat rushed to my cheeks as I stabbed my fork into a heaping plate of pancakes.

"Your naivety amuses us, Princess," Shadow grumbled. "You forget who's house you are in."

I looked down at my plate, humiliated. "I should be getting back to the palace, Lady. Can you please see that my horse is ready by mid-afternoon?"

Lady George pursed her lips. She looked hesitantly between the three lords. "Of course, Princess. I'll see to it at once."

Shadow dropped his fork. It clanked on the table. "Stop. You will do no such thing. The princess stays here."

I jerked my head toward him, fuming. "Don't speak about me as if I'm not in the room. I will leave when I want to."

Lady George murmured something under her breath and scurried out of the room.

"Tulip, my sweet, it's for your own good," Bronte cooed. "We know you don't really want to leave."

"You're just pissed that Shadow beat you at your own game," Ramsay added.

"And we aren't done playing," Shadow snapped.

This was insane. "What in the hell do you want from me?"

Lady George sauntered back in with a tray of eggs and bacon. "Alright, eat up everyone. You're going to need your strength for today."

The three lords looked at me, their expressions blank. Unreadable.

"What in the world are you talking about, Lady?" I asked. Did she have any idea what these sick beautiful Fae men were doing to me? She couldn't be as oblivious as she seemed.

Lady George smoothed her flour coated hands down her apron. "Well, it's our annual garden games, of course. Usually it's just the lords. I'm too old for games. But now they have you to play with."

I nearly choked on a bite of eggs. Ramsay snorted while Bronte laughed inside his napkin. She had no idea how true her words rang.

"Lucky me," I muttered. "What are we playing?"

Shadow leaned back in his chair, looking sexier than I wanted to admit. "You'll see."

There was something wrong with me. Instead of being disgusted, I was turned on. But I wouldn't let them see.

I shoved away from the table and stood. "All three of you… are fucking toxic."

Lady George was putting on her usual façade of pretending she didn't know what was going on between us. She placed a bowl of cherries in my hands. "Winter cherries. They are the sweetest this time of year."

Ramsay cupped my elbow in his hand. "Shall we?"

I cursed under my breath before following them to the garden.

The morning dew trickled off the flowers, freezing before hitting the ground like tiny crystals. The heavy fragrance enveloped me, scents of rose, honeysuckle, and jasmine. It was sweet as it was cloying. So rich it was dizzying.

I looked around to see various lawn games set up—croquet, cornhole, and a large target with a bow and arrows resting against it. A white-clothed table held multiple refreshments. I placed the bowl of cherries on it and picked up a glass of something cold and pink. I took a sip and was pleasantly surprised at the taste. I swirled the tart liquid in my mouth, savoring every drop.

Bronte joined me and did the same. "Ahh, Lady George always did make the best lemonade. The secret is in adding vodka." He winked.

Great. They were going to get me drunk as well.

Ramsay offered me a croquet mallet. I rolled my eyes, refusing to take it.

"What's wrong, Princess?" He asked.

I plopped down on the grass, my pale blue taffeta gown ballooning out around me. "I don't feel like playing your silly garden games."

Shadow picked up the bow and arrows, hitting the target with rapid speed and perfect accuracy. "I knew you were too proper to do anything other than sit and look pretty in the grass."

What the fuck was his problem? A rage bubbled up inside of me. I was not some fragile little doll that they could break so easily.

Jumping to my feet, I snatched the bow out of his hand. "Do you know what princesses actually do, boys?" I pulled the arrow back and locked eyes with Shadow before releasing it. "We train." The wind hissed as my arrow zipped through it, landing in the middle of the target.

I readied another arrow. "Royals are under constant threat. We cannot rely on our guards all the time." The second arrow whizzed through the air and landed next to the first one. "So we train. We learn how to curtsy, which forks go with each course, and which are better for stabbing a man with."

I reached for another arrow, but Ramsay got to it first. "You've made your point, Princess."

Bronte sauntered to my side and wrapped an arm around my waist. "That just made me so hard, Tulip."

I couldn't help but chuckle. His sweetness and boyish charm were impossible to resist. While Shadow pissed me off and Ramsay frustrated me, Bronte was like a breath of fresh air.

I kissed him on the cheek. "Thanks, Bronte. You can watch me shoot things anytime."

For the next few hours I watched the three of them compete with each other, taking turns throwing little sacks into the wooden cornhole board and knocking croquet balls around the lawn. I was on my third lemonade, feeling warm and fuzzy, and realizing how content I was in this moment. The lords laughed and teased each other. Even Shadow seemed to be enjoying himself. My anger was gone, and I had completely forgotten about wanting to escape this place.

I was starting to doze off in the grass when I sensed three dark shadows surrounding me. I peered up through slitted eyelids to find three mischievous stares.

Ramsay lifted me off the ground. "Grab the cherries and follow us." There was an edge in his voice. Something dark and feral.

"Are the games over, my lords?"

Bronte flashed me a toothy grin. "The games are just beginning, sweet Tulip."

Shadow unbuttoned his sleeves and rolled them up, flexing

his muscles. My belly fluttered. As I reached for the bowl of cherries, I downed another pink lemonade. What were they up to now?

The sun was just beginning to set as I followed them to the center of the garden. The fading light cast intricate patterns over the stone fountain. It was beautiful. I sucked in a deep breath. "What are we doing here?"

Bronte took the bowl from my hand and guided me to the edge of the fountain. "It's the winter solstice tonight. A night for rituals and renewal."

I was familiar with the tradition but had never been allowed to partake in the ceremonies. My brother died on a winter solstice. My stepmother hated the holiday and forbid any of us to celebrate it.

"I-I don't want to play anymore." A feeling of dread washed over me.

Ramsay tilted my chin up toward his face. "It is time you reclaim your power, Tallulah. The winter solstice is an ancient Fae tradition. It is your right to own it once again."

I shook my head and backed away from them. "No. I don't deserve to be a part of it. Bad things will happen."

Shadow gripped my shoulders and forced me to sit on the edge of the fountain. He kneeled down to face me. "The past can't haunt you anymore. Not here. Not with us."

I wanted to believe them. To let it all go. But how? "And what will you have me do?"

Bronte smiled. "Nothing. We will feed you, bathe you, and pleasure you under the moonlight."

My eyes brimmed with tears. "Why would you do that for me?"

Ramsay plucked a cherry out of the bowl and sat down next to me. I could feel the spray of water against the back of my neck. "Because you are ours. And we take care of what belongs to us."

I looked at Shadow. His eyes were just as haunted as my soul. "And you want this too?"

He looked down at the ground before holding my gaze again. "It is your right."

I nodded.

Ramsay held a cherry to my lips. "Open up, Tallulah."

As the sweet fruit burst in my mouth, I let out a whimper. "Delicious..."

Bronte untied my corset and slid my dress down to the ground. I perched on the edge of the fountain in nothing but a thin pair of white lace panties. Goosebumps prickled my skin as the cool wind danced around me.

Ramsay took another cherry and swirled it around one of my nipples. I gasped as he took both the cherry and my nipple into his mouth and sucked. I looked down to see my breast dripping in juice as he crushed the fruit between his teeth.

My heart raced and liquid pooled between my thighs.

Bronte kneeled before me and removed my panties, sliding them slowly down my legs. He pushed my legs apart and licked his lips. I let out a moan as he dangled a cherry over my aching pussy. I arched toward him, urging him on.

As he dragged the cherry stem down my slit, I locked eyes with Shadow. He watched me hungrily.

Ramsay peeled back the folds of my pussy. "So wet for us… fuck."

"I'm going to do naughty things to you, Tulip." Bronte took the cherry between his teeth and rolled it over my pussy, massaging it back and forth against my clit.

I bucked as the ridges of his tongue stimulated every nerve as he explored the walls of my pussy. "Yes…oh, fuck."

Ramsay continued to feed me cherries while sucking on my swollen nipples. I threw my head back and looked up at the stars and moon. It was as if they shone only for us tonight. There was an electricity in the air. The magic of solstice.

With each thrust of Bronte's tongue, my orgasm gripped me. I cried out in the night, my voice echoing through the trees like a nocturnal siren. Ramsay squeezed my throat as my juices pooled out of me. Bronte licked my thighs, lapping up every drop of my cum.

I panted, my legs shaking, as Shadow stepped forward. He held a garden hose in his hand. "Bring her here and hold her down."

My heart skipped. I was so aroused I didn't care what he was planning to do. I was willing to let them do anything.

Bronte and Ramsay carried me over to where Shadow stood and laid me down on the cool damp ground. Blades of grass tickled my ass, poking into my crevices. I squirmed in ecstasy as they each pinned one of my arms down.

Ramsay kissed me first, pushing his tongue deep inside my mouth. Then Bronte took my lower lip between his teeth and nibbled, flicking his tongue to my upper lip. Ramsay yanked my head toward his and kissed me hard again. Back and forth they took turns brutally ravaging my mouth. I moaned into it.

Bronte took hold of both my wrists and held them over my head. "Let's get all those sticky juices off of you now, Tulip."

Ramsay inched down and pinned my legs back, spreading me wide open, just as Shadow turned on the hose. A slow trickle of water sputtered out.

I trembled in anticipation. "Oh, gods. What are you doing?"

Shadow kneeled down and held the hose over my belly. I flinched as the cool droplets hit my skin. "It's a bathing ritual," he rasped.

He lowered the hose, hovering it over my slit. The water slid between my folds, and I bucked. "Uhhh…" *Fuck, that felt good.*

Ramsay squeezed my thighs. "Relax and open up for us."

Shadow turned the water down till only a few droplets came out at a time. He pressed the tip of the hose to my clit, and I lost it. A deep guttural orgasm ripped through me. I thrashed under their grip, writhing against the ground as Bronte held my wrists firm. "Oh, you like that, don't you?" Bronte whispered in my ear.

"Do you want more, Princess?" Shadow rasped.

I could barely breathe. "Y-yes," I stammered.

"That's our good girl." I released a blood-curdling moan as he pushed the hose inside of me, his fingers coaxing my folds apart to accommodate it.

My chest heaved as I struggled for air. It was cold and smooth, the tiny droplets of water making me slick and wet.

"Oh, Tulip, you look so fucking hot right now," Bronte breathed. "Move your hips up and down for us."

As Shadow pushed the hose in deeper, I lifted my hips up. "*Fuuuck*," I cried out.

"Yes, Tallulah. Fuck. Just like that. Stretch that tight little cunt for us," Ramsay growled.

I didn't know what was coming over me. Everything about this was dirty and shameful and wrong but it felt so fucking right.

Shadow thrusted it in and out, rubbing the tip of it over my clit each time, dragging it up and down my slit. Each time pushing harder. "I told you I would not be gentle."

The pressure built in my nub, tingles spreading through my entire body as the hose ripped through me. I was sore and raw and aching, but I begged him not to stop. Stars and black spots clouded my vision as I moaned and cried over and over again.

Each wave of pleasure seized my body into a different position as I clenched around the wet rubber hose, twisting and contorting as I came.

I gasped for breath as he slowly pulled it out of me. "How do you feel now that I've rubbed you raw, Princess?" He dragged the tip of the hose up and down my slit as my juices flowed out. "Fuck…I could watch you like this every night."

I whimpered, my legs trembling as Bronte played with my nipples and Ramsay stroked my thighs. "I want every dark and brutal act. Every fucking dirty fantasy you can dream up. Keep breaking me over and over until I can no longer remember a life before you."

Shadow's eyes darkened as the realization hit him that he could no longer decipher who was breaking who. They may be the ones holding me down but deep down he knew I was the one in control. He wanted me with every ounce of his flesh. With every fiber of his being. But if he needed to hide behind his brutality then so be it. I would take him any way I could get him.

CHAPTER 11

The fog was thicker here at Frost Manor. Darker. I pulled the edges of my shawl up higher around my neck as I walked through the mist-covered garden. I passed the spot on the ground where Ramsay had made me cum with a blade of grass and shivered. I crept past the fountain, the garden hose still lying on the ground. After all they had done to me, how could I ever go back to the life I had lived before?

The icy dew on the lavender rose petals tickled my fingers. I ran my hands across the top of them, cooling my heated flesh. I was simmering with ache. The more the lords gave, the more I wanted. It was a need that consumed me. And oh, how I wanted to touch them back. To make them feel even half of what they've made me feel. But it would never be enough.

I followed the cobblestone path around the side of the house, arriving at an open field. Not far off in the distance sat another structure. A barn. A twinge of guilt crept up on me as I remembered my horse. I hadn't seen Wraith since I'd arrived. I hadn't even bothered to check in on him.

The lords wouldn't allow me to return to the palace, but they said nothing of me leaving the main house. My heart raced as I stalked toward the barn. It was midnight, and I was unfamiliar with their land. But I was determined to visit my own horse.

As I neared the barn, a light flickered inside. I hadn't noticed any other servants other than Lady George. And I knew she was fast asleep in her own quarters. Suddenly my pulse quickened. *I shouldn't be roaming around out here in the middle of the night in my dressing gown.*

But my curiosity was getting the better of me.

I kept my pace, head held high, and pushed on the heavy door. It groaned, opening to the shrill sound of cold steel scraping against iron. The scent of straw and wet soil invaded my nose. It was still and quiet, almost pitch-dark. But that little flicker of light drew me farther in.

As I passed each stall and peered inside, my stomach knotted. They were empty. *Who keeps a barn without horses?*

Following the trail of light, I reached a set of wooden stairs. I glanced up, my fingers moistening around the handrail. I was afraid that the darkness would swallow me up and never let me go. But my need outweighed my fear. I sensed someone up there. I could hear their movements. Despite my pounding heart, I wanted to know who.

The stairs creaked as I climbed them, no doubt alerting

whoever was up there of my presence. A rush of adrenaline gripped me, and I took them faster. Better to get the suspense over with before I had a heart attack.

I reached the top and was about to breathe a sigh of relief when the railing bent, knocking me off balance. I cried out as I stumbled onto the landing, my legs twisting underneath me. The air whooshed out of my lungs as my back slammed against the floor.

While blinking away the tiny white stars that threatened to pull me away from consciousness, I saw *him*, looming over me. Tall, chiseled like a god, midnight black hair... green eyes full of violent hunger.

Shadow.

"You're in trouble now, Princess." His voice was smoky, raspy, breathless. Had he been watching me this whole time? Waiting for the right moment to pounce?

I struggled for air. My back ached. "Why are there no horses?"

Shadow snickered. "You always ask the wrong questions." He yanked me up and slammed me against a wooden beam. *"I'm the only beast inside these walls."*

I shuddered. "This is where you sleep, isn't it? I've trespassed into your sacred space. Forgive me. I was just looking for my horse. I'll take my leave now."

I moved to push past him, but he grabbed by arms and pinned them around the beam. I felt the cold press of steel against my wrists, followed by the sound of a click. Oh, no.

He stepped back and smiled. "You're not going anywhere."

I was trapped, my wrists shackled. I should have been

terrified but instead I was deeply and utterly aroused. "I'm not afraid of you," I spat. "Do your worst."

His hand flew to my throat, his fingers digging into my flesh. He growled into my ear, "I plan to."

I clenched my pussy tight. His hot breath in my ear driving me into a frenzy. "Show me who you are, Shadow," I rasped.

He tightened his grip on my throat and ripped my dressing gown open with his other hand. His gaze fell to my swollen nipples. "You will soon regret asking for that."

I sucked in my lower lip, wanting to taste him more than anything. "I'm not as fragile as you think."

Shadow drew circles with this thumb around my nipple. Sweat beaded down my back despite the cold air that drafted in. He watched his own hand touching me, moving from one breast to the other in slow, gentle strokes. But I could see the darkness simmering in his eyes. The monster lingering below the surface. And I wanted every brutal part of him.

I arched my back, whimpering at every touch. *"Take it all out on me..."*

He stilled his hand and then pinched my nipple hard. I cried out, biting my lip as the pain quickly turned to pleasure. He did the same to my other one, and I nearly came. Heat flooded my body as he pressed his chest against mine, almost suffocating me, my nipples aching against the rough fabric of his shirt.

"Listen very carefully, Princess." He squeezed my chin, jerking it up as he gazed down at me. "This isn't a fairytale. You have three seconds to make up your mind. If you stay, you belong to all of us. But right now... you are mine to play with. Mine to fuck. My cock will be the first to destroy that tight wet pussy of yours."

Another surge of moisture pooled between my thighs. My chest heaved with a fury. "Play with me, Shadow."

"One," he grumbled.

"Fuck me," I begged.

"Two."

"*Own me.*"

Another growl rumbled out of him. "*Three.*"

Without warning he flew down the stairs, leaving me naked, breathless, and chained to a beam. I closed my eyes and took a deep breath. What the fuck was I getting myself into? But I couldn't leave. I couldn't walk away. If I did, he would never touch me again. I felt that in my bones. And I needed him inside me like I needed air to breathe.

The minutes ticked by as I waited for his return. The longer I stood there, the more I feared what I was about to receive. Ramsay and Bronte were back at the house, and Lady George was fast asleep somewhere else. I was alone with a monster. But all rational thought was slipping away from me. My body craved his brutality.

The footsteps back up were slower, firmer, and orchestrated to instill fear. I heard him chuckle as he reached the top, followed by a cracking sound. His lips curled into a devious smirk as he faced me. "First, you must be punished for trespassing."

I drew in a sharp breath as I saw what he was holding. A leather riding crop. He tapped it lightly against his palm. I flinched as he came toward me and then dipped around to the back of the beam. His fingers dug into my wrists as he freed my hands.

"Turn around, Princess."

I did as he said, my pulse racing as he yanked me forward and locked my wrists up again. He licked his lips. "You're going to scream so loud."

Shadow dragged the tip of the riding crop across my hips as he inched his way back around. He pressed his hard cock against my ass and whispered, "I'm going to really enjoy marking you."

I shivered as he teased me with it, dragging the crop slowly down the slit of my ass and underneath. I stifled a whimper as he nudged it between my legs, sliding it back and forth. "You know it's only going to sting more now with your juices all over it."

Oh, fuck.

I closed my eyes and hugged the beam. "Just do it."

He hissed as a whoosh of air rushed at me followed by the sharp sting of leather connecting with my ass. "*Ughhh,*" I cried out. My nub vibrated as he brought the crop down again, harder. I lurched forward, the wooden beam scraping my chest.

"*Again.*"

He grunted as he whipped me. The ache, the pain, the lines blurring between pleasure and torture. My wrists burned from the chains. Splinters of wood scratched at my skin as I slid against the beam. I was turned on and horrified. I wanted to heal myself and yet still wear his marks on me at the same time.

This was too much.

Shame was beginning to fester in my belly. My cheeks flushed. How could I want this? There must have been something wrong with me.

"I-I want to go back to my room," I squeaked out.

He placed his hands on either side of me, boxing me in. "No, you don't. You want to stay. Out there, everyone treats you like a fucking princess. And deep down you hate it. But in here… you love being my dirty little whore."

I swallowed hard. Fucking hell. He wasn't wrong. The memory of what his fingers did to me back at the ball. What *he* did to me. I needed to feel that again. But he was feral. An animal. And I was afraid of my own need.

I shook my head. "What else are you going to do to me?"

He took my earlobe between his teeth and whispered, "Whatever the fuck I want."

I cried out as he bit down. "Fuckkk." I tried to jerk away, feeling the wet droplets of blood. "*You bit me.*"

He squeezed the back of my neck. "And you liked it."

"No." I shook my head, and we both knew it was a lie.

He unchained me and spun me around. He shoved a leg in between my thighs, pressing his muscular thigh hard against my nub. I was fucking terrified and yet I had no will to run.

Shadow stood back. He unbuttoned his pants and let them fall to the ground. I gasped at the sight of his massive cock standing fulling erect. "Gods…"

With a smug smirk on his face, Shadow sank into a chair and spread his legs. "Get on your knees, Princess."

I could feel my cheeks flush from shame. "I will do no such thing." And yet I couldn't tear my eyes away from him. I was practically salivating.

"Get the fuck on your knees, or I will throw you to the wolves outside."

"You wouldn't dare."

In one quick grab he reached out and squeezed my throat. "If I have to ask you one more time, Princess, you will find out real soon just what I will dare to do."

I contemplated defying him once more. I wondered how long it would take to get down the stairs before he caught me. And we both knew that I didn't really want to get away.

I lowered myself down between his legs. Before my knees could touch the ground, he fisted my hair and yanked me forward. The pain in my scalp rippled through me as he twisted my head to the side and held me to his bare thigh.

"Look at you now, Princess. Such a dirty little slut for me, aren't you?"

Despite the shame rising to enflame my cheeks, I could not control my arousal. My nipples stiffened as he held me in place.

"Fucking look at you. If the king and queen could see you now. Their innocent little daughter raw and bare for a monster like me."

I looked away, fighting the urge to cry. *What the fuck am I doing?*

He yanked my chin back, so I had to look at him. "Have you ever given a man pleasure before, Princess?"

I felt defeated. Not even sure if he wanted to fuck me or just humiliate me. Or both. "No," I whispered.

Shadow released my head and nudged me up gently. "Do you want to?"

For the first time all night something else blazed in his eyes. More than hunger. *Desire.* Pain was what he was accustomed to, but I had to believe he wanted pleasure too.

I knelt back down and slid my hands up his thighs. "Yes… Tell me what to do."

He sucked in a sharp breath. "Wrap your hands around my cock and lick the tip."

The ridges of his cock pulsed in my palms. Sweat dotted his flesh. Hot like fire. I lashed my tongue out and rolled it over the tip. "Like that?"

He stroked my lips. "*Yes*… Fuck, you look good like that."

Without waiting for his command, I took his cock in my mouth. He gasped and thrusted forward. "That's it, Princess. Slide those pretty lips up and down."

He tasted sweet and salty. A spurt of his cream seeped out and coated my tongue. I moaned as he pulled on my hair, shoving me down farther. I never knew that this act would turn me on so much.

I sucked harder, faster, while he writhed underneath my grip. Shadow was coming undone. And I was the one undoing him.

"Look at me when you devour me."

The second I looked up at him, he thrusted deeper into my mouth. I whimpered as his cock hit the back of my throat. Tears spilled down my cheeks. But I would not stop.

His eyelids fluttered; his gaze feral as we watched each other. My swollen lips rubbing up and down the length of his shaft. His hands tangled in my hair, pulling so hard my scalp burned. I was sick for him. Viciously and brutally obsessed with pleasuring this man.

Shadow jerked my head back, as if reading my mind. "When I cum it will be inside you, Tallulah."

My heart skipped. "I think that's the first time you've ever said my name."

He rubbed his thumb across my swollen lips. "It's a night of firsts, isn't it?" I shivered as he pulled me onto his lap. He brushed my hair back and sucked on my earlobe, still coated in blood from when he bit me.

I moaned as he dipped his fingers into my aching pussy. Shuddering as he whispered, *"I want that cherry now, Princess."*

CHAPTER 12

"How do you want to remember your first time, Tallulah? Hmm? If you're hoping for a sweet love story then you've come to the wrong place. Although, real love stories are often far from sweet. But you already know that. Otherwise you wouldn't be here. So tell me, what do you want to remember?"

I laid naked on his bed, trembling with need, sprawled for his viewing pleasure. "I want to remember *you*. Every dark and vile piece of you. I want to remember that it hurt. That it was ecstasy. That I was afraid, yet happy. That I was safe but in the most dangerous place I could ever be. I want what you want. However depraved or wicked it might be."

Shadow leaned over me and sniffed my neck, growling as he breathed me in. *"What I want is to tear you apart."*

He climbed on top of me and pinned my hands over my head. "And when I'm finally coated in your blood and cum and sweat… I want to lick your wounds clean so I can do it again."

I arched my hips toward him, utterly aroused. The brutality in his voice, the rasp and ache, it was like a lighthouse on a dark stormy night. A beacon lighting my way home. It disturbed and awakened me at the same time.

Shadow sucked in a sharp breath, his lips quivering as if he could already taste me on his tongue. He moved off me, settling by my ankles. "Spread your legs, so I can look at you."

The cotton sheets of his bed cooled the back of my thighs as I opened wide for him. I was burning up, trembling with fear and excitement.

He kneeled between my legs. "Do you want me to ride you like a fucking horse, Tallulah? Will you scream and buck for me?"

"Y-yes," I panted. *"Break me."*

Shadow fisted his cock. He rubbed his thumb over the smooth tip. "Slide one of your fingers down your slit."

My clit swelled as I did what I was told. His gaze turned feral as he watched me. I slid my finger up and down, my insides dripping with need. Aching for release.

He pulled my other hand down. "I want to see you stretch that pussy open. Pinch those lips between your fingers until I tell you to stop."

Oh, fuck. My hands shook as I pulled my flesh back.

Moisture dripped down my thighs. I gripped the edges of my pussy firmly between my fingers.

He slapped my thigh. "Squeeze *harder*, Tallulah. I want to see you red and swollen for me. You cannot feel true pleasure until you've ridden through the threshold of pain."

I whimpered, my legs twitching as I pinched my folds with all my strength. "Ohhh…*fuck*." He knew I would like it. Every command that poured off his lips touched a dark secret place in me. Fantasies that I had never told anyone. And yet *he knew*.

"Such an obedient little whore, aren't you?" Shadow pressed the tip of his cock against my pussy, stilling it there. "*I like that*."

I gasped at the contact. I couldn't help arching up toward it, urging him to put it inside. My pussy throbbed, the delicate lips stinging between my fingers. But it felt so fucking good.

His breath quickened. "Are you ready to let a monster defile you?"

Every inch of my body was starved, my nipples, my clit, every nerve. "I'm ready. Please, Shadow…"

He growled and pushed my hands away. "I want to hear you submit to me. Tell me how bad you want me, Princess."

My heart and my pulse were racing so fast I could barely breathe. Like a switch was turned on inside me, I could not lay there untouched for any longer. "I'm nobody's princess. I'm your dirty little whore. Now fuck me like one."

He inched the tip in a little further, teasing me. "Yes, you are," he rasped. "And now your needy little pussy is going to choke on my cock."

I cried out as he plunged into me. I clenched on instinct as the ridges of his cock burned against my walls, stretching me open. "Uhhhh," I screamed.

A sharp pain stabbed at my back as he pushed himself deeper. I wanted to retreat, to run away from the pain, but he held me firmly in place.

"Relax, Tallulah, open up for me. Remember, pain is the only way through," Shadow whispered in my ear.

"It hurts..." The glass wand and the garden hose didn't even come close to the enormous size of Shadow's cock.

He pressed the full weight of his body against me. His hands roamed my thighs as he kept pushing deeper and deeper into my pussy. It throbbed inside my flesh, long and thick, stretching me wider. The pressure mounted in my belly as if he truly was tearing me apart.

And just when I thought I couldn't take much more, the tension dissipated. "Oh, fuck." My juices pooled, coating his cock, as he began sliding in and out with more ease.

"There we go." He dragged his tongue up my neck and across my jaw. He pulled out slowly before thrusting back in with more force.

I bucked against him, our thighs smacking together in rhythm. I never knew I could feel anything like this. I clenched around his cock, wanting to feel every ridge against my walls.

He wrapped his hand around my throat and squeezed as he leaned back and pounded into me. His feral green eyes sparked with malice and hunger. I held onto his arms as he ripped through me without restraint.

He buried his cock all the way in, pressing on that elusive spot deep inside. Each thrust sent another ripple of pleasure through me. "*Harder*," I begged. I was becoming unhinged. Wild with lust. Greedy for more.

Shadow slapped my thigh and plunged in harder. "Mmm, yes. You love being ripped open, don't you?"

I fisted his hair, pulling his mouth down on mine. He shoved his tongue deep inside my mouth, kissing me violently. "Yes... I want you to ruin me."

I took his lip between my teeth, consumed with lust, and bit down. He let out a deep moan as his blood filled my mouth. The taste of him was ecstasy. There was no going back. I wanted every single brutal piece of him.

He pinched my nipples and stilled his cock. Our gazes locked on each other while his tongue darted out, lapping at the blood on his lips. "I want to play a new game, Tallulah" There was a different edge to his tone. *Something even darker.*

"Yes, whatever you want. Just don't stop." I writhed underneath him, desperate for him to keep fucking me.

Shadow pulled out of me. I gasped at the sight of his cock covered in my blood. "Outside these walls, people bow to you. You command them. But in here... you are mine to do whatever I want with. Do you understand, Tallulah?"

I nodded, breathless. "Yes, Shadow. I'm yours. Now please, I want you back inside me."

He got off the bed and stood over me. "I'm not done breaking you, Tallulah. It's time for you to feel what that's like. And when I'm done, you will cum so fucking hard, the entire kingdom will hear you scream."

I should have been scared but all I could think about was my throbbing clit, the wetness between my thighs, the taste of his blood on my lips. I wanted to be everything for him. To give him whatever he wanted. To let him destroy me so that I could be reborn.

"I am yours to play with, my Lord."

His lips curled into a snarl. "Good," he growled through gritted teeth. "Come with me downstairs."

My heart raced as I followed him down, suddenly remembering where I was. He grabbed my wrist and pulled me into another room toward the back of the barn. "Get on your knees."

I gasped as I glanced around. On the walls hung bridles, saddles, and leather riding crops. There was no bed, no hearth, no warmth. "What are we doing in here?"

Shadow squeezed the back of my neck, guiding me to a tattered rug in the center of the room. He hissed in my ear, "Most people want to tame wild beasts, I prefer to unleash them. Now get on your fucking knees."

Despite my fear, my body sparked with need. I took a deep breath and did as he said. The air was colder in here, darker, and there was a sinister energy that permeated through every crevice of this room. And yet I was more aroused than I'd ever been.

Shadow walked along the wall, fingering each bridle, until he landed on one with thin black leather straps that connected to a pair of reins. He lifted it off the wall and draped it over his arm. "Are you going to obey your lord, Tallulah?"

I shivered as a draft billowed in from underneath the door. My teeth chattered in a mixture of being cold and turned on. "Yes, my Lord," I breathed.

He walked to the next wall and unhooked a black leather

riding crop. "I need you to let go, Tallulah. Nothing else exists except you and me and this room."

He smacked the riding crop against his hand, and I flinched even though he was not yet near me. My first thought was one of horror and shame. Yet as I perched on all fours, naked and coated in blood, a thrill unlike I'd ever known rippled through me.

"Nothing else exists," I rasped.

Shadow knelt down next to me and dragged the tip of the riding crop down my spine. "That's what I like to hear. I'm going to put this on you now." He moved behind me and cupped my ass. "You're going to fucking enjoy this so much. You have no idea."

My arms trembled as I felt the straps of the bridle. He slipped them around my chest and belly, buckling them tight. The leather dug into my skin. My head buzzed as he secured the reins through the metal rings. He gave them a slight tug and I lurched back. "Do you like giving me control?"

For fuck's sake, I was sopping wet. "Yes," I whispered.

Shadow slapped my ass. "Say it again. Who's in control?"

Every inch of my skin prickled. "You're in control, my Lord. I am at your mercy."

He tugged on the reins. "Spread your legs and get lower."

I widened my stance and a soft moan escaped my lips as he rubbed his cock against me. "Do you want me to fuck you like this?"

"Yes," I begged. The anticipation was too much. My adrenaline was spiking. And I needed release.

Without restraint, he thrust his cock deep inside me.

He pulled tight on the reins, forcing me back as he slid in and out. "I've wanted you like this for so long."

My orgasm was already starting to build as the leather straps dug into my flesh. With every violent thrust, I throbbed more.

"Buck for me, Tallulah," he growled.

"Oh, fuck." I drove my hips back as he pulled on the reins.

He cracked the riding crop down against my ass. "*Faster.*"

"*Uhhh,*" I screamed. Pushing off my hands, I rocked back and forth, spreading my legs wider as he filled me. I was so close to exploding all over him. But I didn't want it to stop.

"Told you I would ride you like a fucking horse." Shadow pulled hard on the reins and whipped me again. It wouldn't be long now. I was barely holding it together.

My cheek pressed against the floor as he pushed me down, my arms out in front of me. He slipped a finger inside my ass as he continued to slam his cock inside my needy cunt. I bucked again at the feel of his thick finger exploring between my cheeks. I quivered as he slipped it in and out of my entrance.

"Mmm, Bronte told me you liked that." He yanked the reins back hard with another deep thrust of his cock as he pumped his finger in and out of my ass.

I screamed as the pressure built. The folds of my pussy raw, swollen, as the deepest parts of me roared with animalistic need. I scratched at the floor. "I'm going to cum…"

It spread through me before I even knew what was happening. I screamed as my orgasm took hold. Shadow reached around and squeezed my nipples. "That's it, Tallulah. *Cum fucking hard for me.*"

My cries became a whisper, my throat burning as he rocked in and out. Pressing down on top of me, his lips were on my back, my throat, my shoulders, as he sucked at my flesh, scraping it with this teeth.

"Yes, Shadow. Fuck." I clenched around him as I finally burst. "*Uhhh,*" I screamed. Within seconds, his cum gushed inside me, thick and hot. He released a deep guttural moan, his orgasm gripping him. We rode it out together—me flat on my belly, our juices dripping down my thighs.

I had given him everything. He owned my innocence, my darkest desires, every dirty thought I'd ever had. It all belonged to him in this moment. We laid there for what seemed like hours before Shadow finally shifted his weight off me.

He kissed the back of my neck as he removed the bridle from my back. "You were so good for me, love. So fucking good."

I turned onto my back and pulled him to my side. "Thank you, Shadow."

"You don't need to thank me for making you cum, Tallulah."

Tears brimmed in my eyes. "No," I whispered. "Thank you for giving me all of you. And for letting me be who I really am."

He sighed. "I know all too well what happens to people when they stifle their true nature."

I nestled my cheek against his chest. "That's why you're so angry. You don't have to be anymore. I can be your release."

"You are... you always will be," he murmured.

A calm settled over me. This quiet stillness that I could only ever grasp in my dreams was real. I belonged to them.

Shadow scooped me up off the floor and carried me out of the barn. "Let's go find the others. I've kept you to myself for too long tonight."

I was bruised, bloodied, and swollen. Exhausted. But the thought of sharing myself with Bronte and Ramsay too invoked a carnal lust that could not yet be quenched.

CHAPTER 13

"You're so beautiful," Bronte rasped as Shadow covered me with a blanket and laid me down on the bed. "So perfect."

Ramsay flew to my side. "Is she all right?"

I reached for his hand. "I'm fine. Better than all right."

Shadow nodded. "I've claimed her and now so shall you both."

Bronte's eyes widened. "Are you sure, Tulip?"

I held my other hand out to him. "I want this."

The connection, the energy the three of them radiated was enough to shock me back to life. I had been yearning for acceptance my entire life. Looking for love in strangers' faces and finding only indifference. Until now.

Ramsay's eyes blazed with lust. "Can you handle all three of our appetites?"

This sent another thrill to my core. I shivered, despite the heat spreading between my thighs. My body was alternating between fire and frost. It was a cold winter's night. The barn had been freezing. The night air outside as he carried me, icy. But a fire was simmering beneath my skin.

I moved off the bed, wrapping the blanket around my shoulders as I plopped down onto a purple velvet bench in front of the burning hearth. As I stared into the flames, mesmerized by how they danced with such power and freedom, my emotions welled up inside me. They didn't hide who they were. Every encounter I'd ever had with each of them was pure and raw and bare. I owed them the same vulnerability.

I choked back a sob. "Do you know that I don't think I've ever been loved before? Not since my birth mother died…"

Ramsay and Bronte flew to my side, each taking one of my hands. Shadow leaned against the mantle of the hearth, his gaze burning into mine.

"You're safe with us, Tulip. Let it all out," Bronte whispered.

I breathed out a deep sigh. "I think there was a part of my father that always resented me for her absence. She died giving birth to me. Ironic that I was born a healer and yet I destroyed her on my way into this world… But then, when I was five years old, he met my stepmother and made her his new queen. And they had a son. A beautiful boy with blond curls and blue eyes. I loved him so—" A sob claimed my throat.

Ramsay rubbed my back. "*Own it*, love. Embrace your pain."

I nodded, dabbing at my eyes with the handkerchief

Shadow handed me. "My baby brother loved to splash around in the palace river. I would play with my dolls in the grass while he would toss rocks into the water. The ripples made him giggle. He thought it was magic. I didn't have the heart to tell him otherwise. He loved it so…"

Bronte wiped a fresh tear from my cheek. "It's all right, love. Take your time."

My stomach knotted as the memories came flooding back. "It happened during the winter solstice. Everyone at the palace was busy with planning the festivities. Emmanuel wanted to go to the river, but there was no one to take us. I couldn't bear to see the disappointment on his face. So I scooped him up and snuck out with him. We had done this every day for years. I didn't see the harm in it… But I was so wrong."

Panic rose in my chest as if I were no longer in this room, but back there on the river's edge.

Ramsay tilted my chin up. "What happened next, Tallulah?"

I released a quivering breath. "A winter storm. He was only ankle deep in the river. I had my eyes on him the whole time. But the wind became a hurricane, whipping around us with such force I could barely stand. It dragged him in deeper. I tried to get to him, but I wasn't strong enough. I screamed, but no one could hear me over the festival music… He drowned. And the queen has hated me ever since."

Tears spilled down my cheeks. "*I've hated myself ever since.*"

"That's it love, release it." Bronte caressed my back.

I had never let myself cry over it. I didn't think I deserved to. But now the tears were coming out so hard and fast, I didn't think I could ever stop." It was my fault. I shouldn't have taken him there," I rasped.

Ramsay stroked my cheek. "You were seven years old, Tallulah. If there is blame to be placed, it should be on your parents, the guards, the palace staff even. They should have been watching you and your brother instead of worrying about their lavish party."

Shadow's eyes filled with rage. He knelt down in front of me. "I want to kill them for making you carry this. For ripping your childhood away from you. No child should have to suffer through that."

A warmth spread through me as I looked to each of them. I could feel the pain lifting under their soothing touch and gentle words. But more than anything, I felt acceptance. Belonging. All these years I'd lived with this shame and in one night, they eased a large part of it away from me.

"What did I do to deserve such sweet treatment from you?" I asked.

Ramsay smiled at his brothers and then back at me. "You know why we went to the ball, Tallulah? To see you. It's always been you."

Butterflies danced in my stomach. "What do you mean?"

Bronte squeezed my hand in his. "We were invited to the winter solstice party at the palace all those years ago. We weren't much older than you at the time. Our parents had just passed that morning, and we didn't want to go. But Lady George made us. Said it was our duty to the kingdom. She dragged us there kicking and screaming. We didn't want to celebrate a stupid holiday with a room full of strangers."

"But then we saw you," Ramsay chimed in. "You were crying and screaming at the guards to let you return to your room.
We were dumfounded seeing this tiny little girl slip out of their
grasp."

Shadow chuckled, his eyes lighting up in a way I'd never
seen. "We watched as you pummeled them with cakes and ber-
ries, flitting in between them in your bare feet like you were
possessed by the gods themselves. We laughed so hard... *You*
did that for us, Princess. On one of the worst days of our lives,
you gave us something to smile over. Something to hope for...
A wild unhinged girl with fire in her heart. We've loved you
ever since."

My mouth dropped open. I was speechless. *They loved me.*
This entire time when I thought I was all alone, these three
beautiful Fae men loved me from afar. They had been waiting
for me. Another memory flashed in my mind. I let out a gasp.

"I remember. For so long, all I clung to from that day was
the river. But I remember now. The queen was dragging me
away. I looked back to stick my tongue out at the guards, and
I saw you. Three black-haired, green-eyed boys, laughing un-
controllably. I was so angry. I thought you were laughing *at* me."

Ramsay smoothed a strand of hair back from my face. "No,
love. We were in awe of you. We knew you would be ours someday. These years without you have been agony."

I had always felt like something was missing. And now I
knew it was them. They were mine, and I was theirs. "I choose
all three of you as my mates. I don't care if I lose my crown or
get banished from the kingdom. I will not be without any of
you ever again."

"No one will take you from us. I'll kill anyone who dares," Shadow growled.

His possessiveness stirred an ache in me. My nipples pebbled under the blanket. "You asked me earlier if I can handle your appetites. Can you handle mine?"

Shadow stretched back against the hearth. "Tell us what you want, Princess."

I pulled the blanket away from me and tossed it on the floor. "I want you to watch Ramsay and Bronte defile me. Just as you defiled me in the barn tonight. I want to be claimed by all three of you."

A devilish smirk played out on his lips as his eyes trailed over every inch of my naked flesh. "Let the show begin."

Bronte moved behind me. He inched his hands slowly down my chest. I rested my head back against him as he rubbed my swollen nipples between his fingers. "Mmm, my little Tulip," he breathed in my ear. "Spread your legs, darling."

Ramsay knelt down in front of me as I parted my thighs. I arched back, whimpering, as he peeled back the lips of my pussy. He dragged a finger down my slit. "Shadow may have popped your cherry, but now I'm going to taste it."

An ache stirred in my gut as I watched him suck my virgin blood off his finger. "Fuck…" His eyes blazed with hunger. "I want more."

Bronte spun me sideways, so I was laying down on the length of the bench. He pressed my shoulders down into the soft velvet while Ramsay perched himself at the other end. The desire was overwhelming. I wanted nothing more than this.

Ramsay pushed my legs wider apart, each one dangling

over the bench, and scooted me down to the edge. "Hold her wrists, brother. I want to see our princess squirm."

A thrill rippled through me as Bronte pinned me down.

"Play with her nice and slow. *Torture her*," Shadow rasped as he watched on.

Ramsay chuckled as he lowered his mouth between my legs. I flinched as his tongue darted out against my clit.

Bronte pressed my wrists hard against the bench. "Do you like when I restrain you, Tulip?"

"Yes," I panted.

Ramsay circled my nub with his finger, sliding it up and down my entrance. "So wet for us."

I cried out as he plunged the length of his tongue inside my pussy and held it there, flicking it back and forth against my walls. He pinched my clit between his fingers as he pulled out. "*Fuck*, you taste good."

The tingling spread like wildfire through my whole body. I couldn't breathe. I jerked away from Bronte on instinct, wanting my hands free to claw at Ramsay's skull but his grip was too strong. And it only turned me on more. I bucked and writhed as Bronte squeezed my wrists tighter. I felt like a wild animal.

"Yes, sweet Tulip, fight me. It will make you cum even harder," Bronte whispered in my ear.

"Oh, fuck," I cried out.

Ramsay scraped his teeth across my thighs and back to my sopping wet folds. He licked and sucked and nibbled on every single inch of my pussy, devouring me like a hungry beast. The pressure in my nub began to build as the tingling increased.

Shadow let out a soft moan. I turned my head to see him

fisting his own cock. He stroked his veiny shaft up and down, coating himself with his own juices. I licked my lips, wanting to taste him. "Shadow, come closer."

He growled and rushed over to me.

Ramsay thrusted his tongue deep inside my pussy, pulling my attention back toward him. I cried out as he hit my special spot. Each flick coaxing my orgasm out of me.

I kept my eyes glued to Ramsay, but I needed more. "I want to taste you, Shadow... give me every drop," I managed to mumble out.

Shadow stroked his cock faster.

Bronte panted over me. "Such a good little whore for us. Letting us share you." He took one of my nipples between his teeth and gently bit down."

I screamed as pain, then pleasure flooded me. I was done for. "I'm cum...cum—" I unleashed a bloodcurdling cry as my orgasm took hold of me, seizing my body into a twisted state of ecstasy.

Bronte held firm as I bucked and jerked against Ramsay's mouth. "Ohhh, fucckkk."

"Open wide, Princess." Shadow straddled my face as he rubbed his cock. As soon as the tip of his cock slapped against my tongue, he released, grunting, and growling as his cum rushed down my throat in thick hot ropes. I lifted my head so as not to choke and clamped my lips tight around his shaft.

I sucked and swallowed Shadow's sticky white cream with Ramsay's tongue still lodged deep inside me. I didn't know what to focus on except that every part of me was over stimulated to the utmost degree. Every orgasm ripped from me, rolled into the next.

But it wasn't enough. I was insatiable when it came to them.

It took me a moment to realize Bronte had released my wrists. They were raw and numb from the pressure. I sat up, licking the remaining traces of Shadow's cum from my lips. The three of them gaped at me, wild-eyed.

I reached out to Bronte and Ramsay. "I want to feel you both at the same time."

"Fuck, Tallulah, you are a beast," Shadow praised. He curled his arm around the bedpost while Bronte and Ramsay both stripped out of their clothes.

My heart raced as I drank in the sight of their taut chiseled bodies. Their cocks erect and eager to fill my needy pussy.

I pushed Bronte onto the bed and straddled him. Ramsay nestled in behind me. "Remember, Princess, own it. *Own us.*"

Still slick from Ramsay's tongue, I lowered myself onto Bronte's hard cock. We both gasped as I slid my pussy down. "That's it, baby, stretch for me."

Oh fuck. I was raw and swollen but it felt so fucking good. Each ridge tickled my insides, stoking the fire that Shadow had started in the barn.

I rolled my hips, thrusting hard against him. And as Bronte pulled out, Ramsay yanked me back and thrusted his cock deep inside my pussy. A shuddering moan escaped me as he pounded into me.

Shadow moved to the side of the bed and grabbed my chin, tilting it toward him. "Look at me while they fuck you."

Ramsay pulled out of me and shoved me back toward Bronte. I let out another cry as Bronte entered me again. I was on fire. Aroused to the point of blacking out. My juices streamed down my thighs. "Fuck you are so wet," Bronte growled. "Ride me, Tulip. I don't want you to be able to sit down for a week."

Shadow reached in between us and rubbed my clit. "Who do you belong to, Princess?"

The tension between my thighs was building as we moved back and forth in perfect rhythm. As soon as Bronte would pull out, Ramsay would thrust in. I shuddered as my orgasm began to climb.

Ramsay slapped my ass hard as I ground against Bronte. "Answer him, Tallulah."

I bit down on my lip to stifle a cry. "I belong to you. All three of you own me."

Bronte steered my hips down hard. We both cried out as he throbbed against my walls, his cum filling me to the brim. It sent me over the edge. I clenched as the tingling pierced me deep inside and fluttered out in waves. I rubbed my nub against him, milking it for every drop. "Fuck..."

Before I could catch my breath, Ramsay yanked me back. "*My turn,*" He growled in my ear.

I screamed as the ridges of his cock tore through me, rubbing me raw. But just when I thought I'd had enough, it sent me into a frenzy, my climax building again. Ramsay pounded into me hungrily, violently, and without restraint. Blood and cum dripped down my thighs.

"Ramsay... *harder*. Please." I was completely and utterly consumed by them. The pain, the pleasure, it was one and the same, and I needed both.

"Such. A. Good. Fucking. Whore." He thrusted deeper and harder with each word that left his lips.

A fresh orgasm rippled through me as his hot liquid splashed against my swollen flesh. "*Yes*," I moaned.

Ramsay dug his thumbs in between my ass cheeks as he stilled his cock. I could feel him throbbing against me as every drop of his cum emptied out. The tingling in my nub trickled down my slit and to my backside. I rocked into it as he played with my ass.

"Do you like that, Tallulah? Hmm? You like when I touch you here?" Ramsay stroked my anus in a slow circular movement.

My eyes rolled back, and I couldn't even form sentences.

Bronte chuckled and moved out from underneath me. "Her pretty pink nipples are telling me she does." He stroked my breasts as Ramsay continued to knead his thumb deeper into my ass. My mouth watered and a rumbling stirred in my abdomen. On my knees, naked, panting, and surrounded by three wicked deviants, I felt feral.

Ramsay drew in a sharp breath. "Unclench for me, Tulip... I'm almost all the way in."

Shadow ran his fingers through my hair. "Relax, Tallulah. Let him get nice and deep like you want him to."

My breath quickened as I slid my legs farther apart,

lowering myself closer to the bed. What was happening to me? This need for them to fill me was obsessive. It was indecent and depraved, but it was mine. *They were mine.*

"That's it. Now you're opening up for me." Ramsay slid his thumb in deeper, and I bucked. I fisted the sheets as he pushed gently in and out.

"Oh, gods. Fuck. Don't stop," I panted. I clenched as another orgasm gripped me. The three of them caressed my back as I unleashed everything I had. It all bubbled up and ripped out of me in one single blood curdling scream.

CHAPTER 14

There was a darkness in me, leading me here this whole time. A pull like a magnet that drew me to this place. To them. And I would not let them go.

I stood in front of the mirror and really looked at myself for the first time. I was different. I smiled as my gaze traveled over the bite marks and the bruises. The rope burns on my wrists, handprints on my neck… I could heal them in seconds. Snap my fingers and make them disappear as if they were never even there. But instead I wanted to admire them. These were their marks on me. And I would wear them like tattoos until they faded away on their own. Until they marked me again.

Lady George hummed a sweet tune as she flitted around

the breakfast table, pouring coffee and laying out colorful little cakes. "Ah, good morning, Princess. Did you sleep well?"

Stifling a laugh, I took a seat at the table. I had slept better than I'd ever had but only because Ramsay, Bronte, and Shadow had worn me out. "Very well, Lady. Thank you."

My stomach grumbled as the scent of sugar and flaky dough hit my nose. I helped myself to a few pastries, not wasting anytime on sinking my teeth into one. "Delicious," I murmured through bites.

"You certainly are," Ramsay drawled as he entered the room.

Shadow and Bronte followed, taking their seats across from me. Their gazes trailed over my marks, pleased that I'd kept them. There was no more reason for me to dress modestly. I had chosen a low-cut pink corset, the top lined with tiny little rose buds and the laces were ribbons made from the finest Fae silk. My pink skirt was gathered in bunches, like the bottom of a ball gown, and rested low on my hips to expose my midriff. Shadow seemed especially pleased with that.

"The palace has been looking for you, Princess," Lady George announced. "A footman traveled through here last night, but I sent him away. Told him, I hadn't seen you."

Fear crept into my chest. That would explain why they hid my horse from the start. "I must return today. Before the queen changes her mind about letting me choose my own mate."

"We're going with you," Bronte rasped.

Shadow and Ramsay both nodded in unison.

"They might not understand... I should try to talk with them first." I was terrified to be away from my mates, but I didn't want to get them thrown into the palace dungeon either.

Lady George cleared her throat. "Forgive me, Princess, but I know a thing or two about royal decree. There is a very old law that states a royal may choose as many mates as they like. It hasn't been invoked in centuries, but it is there nonetheless."

At that, the four of us perked up. If that were true, than the queen would not be able to stop me. "Are you sure of this, Lady?"

She nodded. "Quite. It is part of my duties to know these things. Return together and claim them as yours. Do it publicly. They will have no choice but to accept it or else risk breaking their own laws."

A flicker of excitement trickled through me. "You must come with us, too, Lady. As a witness, and as a maid of my court. We will live in the heir's palace together."

Lady George beamed. "I would like that very much, Princess. I've raised these lads from a very young age. I would like to remain with them until I take my last breath."

Ramsay chuckled. "Of course, you'll stay with us, George. It's not even a question. Your last breath is a tad dramatic, isn't it?" he teased.

She narrowed her eyes at him. "I'm an old woman, Ramsay. I can't stick around here forever."

Bronte sighed. "You're right. We are kind of tired of you."

Lady George gasped and threw a biscuit at him. Bronte ducked, laughing as she cursed under her breath.

I hadn't seen this playful side to them before. It filled me with so much joy. The thought that we could have this every morning. It was all I wanted. A family that truly loved each other.

"It's settled then. I'll prepare the carriage and the horses. We'll leave in an hour." Shadow stood and came around to my chair. He leaned down and whispered in my ear, "I can't wait to defile you in every room of the palace."

My pulse quickened, awakening my carnal hunger for him. For all three of them. I sucked in a sharp breath. "Promise?" I asked coyly.

He kissed my cheek, letting his lips linger over my skin before pulling away. "Always."

"Go help your brother, boys. The princess and I will meet you out front shortly."

And just like they were children again, they obeyed and took their leave.

I covered her hand with mine. "Please, call me Tallulah. Princess is much too formal, and we are way past that."

She smiled. "As you wish, but it will take some getting used to."

A pinch of fear twisted in my gut. Happiness seemed to be so fleeting for me in my life. It was hard to believe that I was going to get what I wanted. "Do you really think they will accept this ancient law? What if this angers them? I would die if anything happened to my lords.

Lady George shook her head as she cleaned up the table. "They wouldn't dare. Besides, the Frost boys hold deeply dark magic in their veins. Their reputation is widely known in the kingdom. If the king and queen refuse your wishes, Ramsay,

Bronte, and Shadow will whisk you out of there so fast, the court won't know what happened."

Mine. They were mine. And they would protect me. Defend me. I was almost drunk on the euphoria of it. That feeling of knowing that those three beautiful and strong men would literally kill for me. It should frighten me, but all it did was make me love them more.

"Then I have nothing to fear," I murmured.

She winked at me. "You needn't be afraid ever again."

I helped Lady George finish clearing the table and headed toward the door. I hadn't arrived with any belongings except the magic that pulsed through my veins. "My horse, Lady? Is Wraith all right?"

"Of course, dear. Ramsay will bring him round with the other horses. Now magic yourself a warm cloak. There's a crisp chill in the air out there."

I nodded, snapping my fingers, and was immediately covered by a thick black wool cloak. I pulled the hood up around my blonde hair and gave the foyer one last look. With any luck, we'd be at the heir's place this time tomorrow night. But oh, how I loved this manor. I found myself within its very walls.

With a deep breath and a final look around, I stalked out the front door to my new destiny.

By the time we reached the palace, it was raining so hard I could barely make out the road in front of us. The guards at the gates eyed me warily as if they knew trouble had been brewing in my absence. They nodded and waved us through with only a beat of hesitation. I took a deep breath through my nose and willed myself to not get sick. The notion of facing my stepmother was becoming all too real as our carriage bounced across the cobblestones. Memories of her power, how she's used it to hurt me, came flooding back.

My lords surrounded me in a protective bubble upon exiting the carriage. Lady George trailed behind us, humming joyfully as she did. But she was slightly off key, hinting at her own apprehension in this unusual turn of events.

Another set of guards stood at the main entrance to greet us, offering me a slight nod of respect despite the fact that I held no real power here. I might be the king's daughter, but my stepmother was the one they truly feared.

I started forward, but Ramsay held me back. "Remember who you are, Tallulah. Own it."

He looked so sure of himself. They all did. I gazed upon all three of their faces, in awe of how strong and beautiful they were. Mesmerized at their unwavering loyalty to their broken princess that they had only just met. And yet I had to remind myself that they had loved me since I was a child. I was still letting that seep into my veins. They had been waiting for me.

Shadow's eyes darkened, his black pupils threatening to overtake every spec of green. "And remember who we are. You are our concern. Our mate. And we will not allow anyone, not even the queen, to harm you in any way."

I forced a smile at an attempt to appear more confident,

but I was trembling inside. "I pray to the gods that it will not come to that."

Bronte planted a soft kiss on my cheek. "You walk in there with your head held high, Tulip. Like the exquisite flower you are."

I nodded and stepped forward, pushing down all my doubts and insecurities. As we entered the great hall, I locked eyes with the queen. She sat next to my father in their oversized throne chairs. Even from this distance, I could see the contempt on her face.

And with each step I took, my mates flanking me, I grew angrier. The queen had stolen my childhood, placed the burden of my brother's death on me, and was now forcing my hand into marriage under the guise of choice. Well, her abuse ends today. I may have healed all the scars on the outside, but I still carried the pain of her torture in my heart.

Lady George scurried up from behind me to walk in step. She squeezed my hand in assurance. A simple gesture that meant so much in this moment. Another reminder that I was no longer alone.

As we neared, the scowl on my stepmother's face deepened. She rose from her chair. "Where in the gods have you been, Tallulah?"

My father glared at each of my mates before narrowing his hardened gaze on me. "We have been worried sick about you, child. What have these men done to you?"

I started to speak but the queen's malicious laughter cut me off. "Isn't it obvious, husband? Your daughter has been galivanting around the kingdom like a common whore."

Whispers and murmurs broke out amongst the crowd that was slowly gathering in the hall—a mixture of palace staff, guards, low level royals, and even some commoners who were there to pay their monthly taxes. My mates tightened their circle around me, their breaths collectively quickening. But the queen's words meant nothing to me. It was in that moment that I realized she was jealous. Envious of my youth and freedom. It drove her mad to look at me and see my mother in me. Because if she saw it, so did my father. And he would have never married this awful woman if my mother were still alive. Every time she looked at me, I reminded her of that.

"Easy, my Lords. Her words cannot hurt me anymore," I whispered.

I stepped forward and gave a slight bow. "Forgive me, Your Highnesses, I should have sent word of my absence. As you can see, I'm perfectly fine, and I've brought word of my betrothal."

The queen scoffed. "You left the palace without permission. Without a royal escort. And judging by the way these three are salivating over you, my guess is you have been highly indecent in your escapades."

That drew a chuckle out of me. "And yet you dressed me like a common whore for the ball in hopes that I would ensnare a husband of your choosing. You only wanted me to believe I had a choice. It is only indecent if it's unwarranted. I am not a child anymore. You saw to that a long time ago. But I stand before you now, as a woman. And I have come to announce who I shall marry."

A collection of gasps rang out across the room.

Ramsay snickered. "That's right, Tulip. *Claim your power.*"

"Allister," the queen cried to my father. "Are you going to sit here and allow her to speak to me this way?"

The king sighed, his forehead creasing. "She is not wrong, my Queen. It is our fault this happened. We placed too many burdens on you, Daughter. Speak your mind, Tallulah. Which one of these men have you chosen as your mate?"

I smiled at Ramsay, Bronte, and finally, Shadow. I was surer of our love than I had ever been about anything. "All three of them."

Another eruption of gasps and murmurs broke out amongst the ever-growing crowd.

My stepmother looked as if she were about to crawl out of her own skin. She twisted and writhed in her throne chair like a caged animal. "Have you lost your mind, Princess? Allister, please do something before your spoiled brat of a daughter puts me in an early grave."

"That can be arranged," Shadow snarled.

The queen's guards closed in around her.

I put my hand on his shoulder. "That won't be necessary, my love."

The king held up his hand for the guards to still. "Tallulah… I know I haven't been the best father. Someday when you wear the crown you will see how difficult it is to be both leader to your kingdom and parent to your child. I know you're acting out, and I deserve that. But please be reasonable. You cannot take three husbands."

A satisfying smirk crawled across my lips. "Oh, but I can. And I will."

The king groaned, shaking his head.

Lady George stepped forward and bowed. "If I may speak, Your Highness?"

"And who in the gods are you, woman?" the queen snapped.

She lifted her chin proudly. "I am Lady George, keeper of House Frost, and caretaker to the lords of Frost Manor. I have studied the laws of this kingdom since I was a young girl. It has been my duty. I've come to ensure that our most sacred laws are upheld."

The queen snarled at her. "And you think you know our laws better than us? The King and Queen of Cinder Falls?"

Lady George smiled. "With all due respect, Your Highness... yes."

The crowd wasn't bothering to whisper anymore. The noise in the hall rose as what seemed like a thousand conversations were being had at once.

"Silence!" the king yelled as he pounded his jeweled cane against the floor. The crowd fell into an instant hush. "I am well aware of which law you are hinting at. But it hasn't been invoked in centuries."

I inched closer to the throne. "But it *is* a law, Father. Which means I am well within my right to invoke it. You said I had a week to choose a mate. That I had to pick someone from the ball. Well, I have. Ramsay, Bronte, and Shadow were all in attendance. And I choose them. Whether I have your blessing or not. I can either rule with them by my side, or not rule at all. That is the only part of this that you have a choice in… Your Highness."

"Allister, I will not stand for this." The queen was up out of her chair again.

"What will you have me do? Lock her up? Force her to marry someone else after we promised her a choice? She is our only heir." The king could not hide the sadness in his voice.

"And who's fault is that?" the queen spat. "If she had only done what she was told to begin with, my baby boy would still be here."

A lump welled in my throat. "Enough," I yelled, causing everyone's eyes to widen at my newfound voice. "I am tired of carrying the weight of my brother's death on my shoulders. The burden *you* placed on me when I was only seven years old. It wasn't fair then and it's not fair now. I loved Emmanuel more than anything. And I live with the guilt of his death every day. But no more. It was a terrible and horrific accident. I think I have been punished enough."

Black smoke began to swirl around the queen's clenched fists. She started toward me; her eyes feral. My mates pushed me back, forming a line in front of me. Thick smoke began to seep out of their own fingertips. Fuck. I had hoped this could be settled without bloodshed. Without dark magic. But deep down I knew the queen would never be reasonable.

As my mates' magic swirled toward the queen's, I noticed my own magic seeping out. But it wasn't the same. I turned over my palms and instead of white sparks of light, silver and gold tendrils snaked out, laced between black coiling ribbons. *What the hell?*

My heart hammered as it reached for Ramsay first, joining his. I watched, breathlessly as it moved to Bronte, wrapping itself around his fingers gently like a soft blanket. Tingles spread throughout my body as it enveloped Shadow. The tendrils darkened, becoming a sea of black smoke and silver sparks. I felt them. All three of them. I physically felt their magic in my bones.

Lady George whispered. *"You are one."*

The king and queen looked on in shock, their eyes wide and mouths gaping. The crowd backed away toward the doors. Even the guards were unsure of what to do as they glanced nervously back and forth between us and the throne.

My father suddenly stood. His hand trembled as he leaned on his cane. "All this time… I thought you didn't inherit any of my magic. But here you are, wielding it. You are a healer *and* a destroyer. Remarkable."

"Is it though?" The queen snickered.

He glared at her. "Sit down, Griselda."

She obeyed but kept me in her sights.

As I dropped my hands and pulled my magic back, my mate's paused for a second before doing the same.

Lady George stilled a hand on my shoulder. "Perhaps it was stifled, Your Highness. When a child has to constantly heal themselves with their magic, that doesn't leave much space left for anything else."

A chill crawled up my spine. She was right. I had spent

so much of my life, my energy, healing the wounds inflicted on me, that I never had a chance to see what else my magic was capable of. I had thought that there was something wrong with me. Why had I only been gifted my mother's magic, but not my father's?

I turned to my mates. "You knew, didn't you? You lured me away from here, so I could see…"

Bronte kissed my forehead. "We saw it in you all those years ago."

"But we knew it would never manifest until you got away from this miserable palace," Ramsay added as he stroked my back.

Shadow took my hands in his. "I had to get you angry, Tallulah. Angry enough to leave here and seek us out."

Tears streamed down my cheeks before I could stop them. "That's why you didn't want me to heal myself. You wanted me to own my darkness."

Shadow pulled me to his chest, and whispered, "Yes, love. But I do enjoy seeing our marks on you."

This was more than love. More than lust or deviant games. They were my mates. My true family. I turned back toward my father. "Will you accept my decision?"

As the crowd began to chatter again, the king tapped his cane on the ground. "I have underestimated you, my daughter. For that, I am truly sorry. My choices have caused you so much pain and heartache. That ends today. By the power of the crown that I wear upon my head, and the true law of Cinder Falls, I declare your decision worthy and legitimate. I honor you with the heir's palace for you and your three husbands. Upon the birth of your first child, I will place my crown upon your head. And the kingdom will be yours."

I released the breath I'd been holding as a cry wrenched from my throat. "Thank you, Father."

My mates encircled me as the queen again rose from her chair. The entire room seemed to clench in fear as she glared at me. "Well played, Tallulah. Perhaps you'll make an excellent queen after all." And with that she spun on her heel, but not before shooting my father a murderous glare.

The king gave me a nod. "I'm proud of you, Daughter. May you finally find the joy and love you truly deserve."

I beamed back at him. "I already have, Father."

Ramsay, Bronte, and Shadow knelt before me and took turns kissing my hands. As they rose, each one placed a set of cuff links in my palm.

"Shall we go christen our new home, Tulip?" Bronte winked.

Heat flooded my belly. "Yes, my Lords," I rasped.

"There are so many things we have yet to show you," Shadow growled in my ear.

Ramsay trailed his thumb across my lips. "So many more games to play, Princess."

Moisture pooled between my thighs. "And I have some games of my own, my Lords."

Lady George was already shaking her head and walking three steps ahead of us. "I'm going to ride up front," she grumbled.

The four of us burst out laughing as we followed her back to the carriage. As we rode away, my heart felt lighter. I had gotten more than just my freedom. I had found my truth, my love, and my magic.

And I owed it all to three little Fae boys who grew up waiting for me to claim my power. *To claim them.* I gazed at them in awe, in love, and with desire as we rode to our new home. To our destiny.

"You know you can't be queen until one of us puts a child in your belly," Ramsay teased.

"Shall we start trying now?" Bronte dragged his tongue across my jaw.

My nipples pebbled as Shadow sucked on my earlobe. "The sooner the better. Don't you agree, Princess?"

I sucked in a sharp breath as Ramsay hiked my skirt up and pushed my legs apart. He pulled my panties to the side. "Look how wet she is for us."

A moan escaped my lips as both Bronte and Shadow pulled back the lips of my pussy. Ramsay licked the length of my slit slowly, coating his tongue in my juices. I leaned my head back and closed my eyes.

Shadow rubbed my swollen clit, stroking it so achingly, it was all I could do not to cum at the slightest touch. Bronte sucked on my nipples, gently scraping his teeth across them, sending tiny shivers over my flesh. I quivered in their hands, surrendering to their control. Ramsay thrust his tongue inside my pussy, planting kisses on my folds as he slid in and out.

I bit down on my lower lip as the pressure in my nub throbbed. It fluttered through the insides of my flesh, claiming me. Owning me.

"Who do you belong to, Tallulah?" Shadow growled.

"You, my Lords. I belong to the three of you."

As the waves of my orgasm seized me, all I could think about was our love. I cried out and tendrils of my magic wrapped around them, pulling them closer, deeper, as their hands and tongues caressed me.

They showered me with kisses as I rode my pleasure to its peak.

We would be like this forever. Nothing could keep us apart ever again. Not even the chimes of wicked midnight.

EPILOGUE

"Keep your eyes closed, Mommy!" Aurora giggled. Tiny fingers pulled at my own as my girls led me outside.

"She's going to be so happy," Scarlett squealed. The sound of their voices made my heart burst with love. It was the sweetest sound I'd ever heard. And it never grew tiresome. Even when they were fighting over their dolls or shrieking through the palace like wild animals.

"Almost there, Mom, *keep* your eyes closed," Crimson ordered. She was the more serious one of the three. Always so stoic and poised. She had so much of my mother in her. Oh, how I wished they could have known their grandmother.

The summer wind danced across my face, bringing scents of

freshly cut grass, honeysuckle, and jasmine. This was my favorite time of year. I had spent all winter by the palace fire counting down the days till we could frolic by the river.

"Now be a good little whore and do as your told," Ramsay whispered in my ear, teasingly.

I gasped. "Ramsay, *quiet*."

"Relax, my Queen. No one can hear me or that racing heart of yours."

"There's plenty of time for that later, brother. Don't want to get our queen too worked up to enjoy her surprise," Bronte quipped.

I knew this palace like the back of my hand. I didn't need to see to know we were at the river. The ripples of the water were like music to my ears. It had taken a long time for me to finally love being here again. To replace all the bad memories with good ones. But with the help of my mates and our children, my favorite place was given back to me.

"Open your eyes, my love," Shadow cooed.

The light blinded me for a second as I took in our surroundings. I glanced around, taking in the river, the grass, and then… A sob lodged in my throat as I saw it. My knees buckled. Ramsay and Shadow flew to my side and held me up.

"Do you like it, love?" Bronte asked.

There, at the edge of the river, was an enormous statue. A scene frozen in time forever. It was us. Me and my brother. The most exquisitely carved bronze likeness of me as a little girl, playing with my dolls, and Emmanuel next to me, a wide smile on his face as he skipped rocks in the river.

My hands trembled. "It's… beautiful."

143

"Why are you crying, Mommy?" Scarlett asked.

Shadow picked her up and threw her on his shoulders. "Sometimes tears can mean you're happy, little wolf."

I wiped my tear-stained hands on the grass. "Other than our children, this is the most special thing anyone has ever given me. Thank you." I kissed each of my mates on the cheek. "You are too good to me."

We embraced as we watched our girls hold hands around the statue, giggling and singing. Their long black curls bouncing around them as they danced, their eyes sparkling, green like their fathers. We didn't discern which one belonged to who. We didn't want to know. They were ours. That's all that mattered. And we loved them all the same.

Ramsay fingered the back of my neck. "Shall we fetch Lady George to occupy the children? I'm in the mood for a few games."

No matter how much time passed, or how many deviant wicked games we played, I was just as hungry for their touch as the first time.

Shadow nodded. "But where should we defile you this time? Hmm? The royal barn perhaps."

Bronte gripped my waist from behind. "Or maybe we could have some fun in the dungeons."

I shivered, the ache between my legs growing. "I do need to properly thank you for my gift," I cooed.

The three of them chuckled as we gathered the girls and raced back to the main house. Lady George was already waiting for us at the entrance. "Come on girls, let's go eat cake for dinner and play with dark magic." She winked at me.

I snorted. "Very funny, Lady."

The four of us looked on in adoration at these beautiful little angels we'd created. It was hard to tear ourselves away, even as our appetites for each other grew.

But I finally let them lead me away, down to one of our *special* rooms. As soon as they locked the door behind us, I stripped out of my gown and spread out across the bed, eager for each one of them to fill me.

"I think tonight's the night. Don't you think?" Ramsay asked.

I nodded. "Yes, I'm ready."

I mounted Shadow as he laid on the bed. I stroked his shaft as I lowered my throbbing pussy onto it. "Oh, yes…*Uhhh*," I moaned as he twitched inside me.

He dug his fingers into my ass, spreading my cheeks apart. "Take a deep breath, love."

We had been working toward this for months. And now I was slick with need. Bronte stroked my back as Ramsay came up from behind. He squirted lubricant down my folds, rubbing it in deep with his fingers, massaging it in. I stilled over Shadow as Ramsay pushed at my other entrance.

"So wet for me, fuck, Tallulah. I'm going to cum before I even start," Ramsay rasped.

I cried out as he pushed his cock inside my ass.

Shadow grunted as he moved in and out of my pussy. "You're doing so good taking both of us."

The pressure in my belly grew as they fucked me from both sides. I rocked back and forth between them, feeling every inch of their cocks inside of me throb and pulse.

Ramsay burst inside of me, trembling as he came. Without wasting any time he pulled out and Bronte took his place.

Shadow cried out as I rode him harder. *"Such a good fucking queen."*

Bronte's cock pierced my entrance. With Ramsay's thick cream making it easy for him to slide in, he thrusted in hard. I bucked as he pounded into me.

Ramsay grabbed my head and yanked me toward his cock. "Taste what you did to me, Tallulah."

I let out a quivering moan as he shoved his cock into my mouth. Shadow thrusted harder into my pussy while Bronte defiled my ass, ripping and stretching it open as he rode me. We were one unit, obsessed with consuming each other. They both came undone together, filling me from both sides. I was drenched. Coated in cum, sweat and blood. An orgasm unlike any I'd ever known radiated through me, reaching deep into the depths of my body. I tore away from Ramsay and let out a scream. The three of them surrounded me, wrapping their arms around me like a cocoon. This was our life together. It was beautifully twisted and messy and perfect.

All was right in Cinder Falls again. We ruled together, me and my three deviant kings. Someday, our girls would find mates of their own. Mates of their own choosing. But for now, they would have the childhood that we never had. And we would have the life we'd always desired. A life without shame. One filled with love, and laughter, and hope.

OTHER BOOKS BY
M VIOLET

Good Girl (A Dark Romance Novella)

ACKNOWLEDGEMENTS

Thank you for reading *Wicked Midnight*.

Thank you to my AMAZING street team, M Violet's Vixens and Villains! I would not be where I am without you. The messages, videos, and art you send me literally breathe life into my creative well and fill my little Gothic heart with so much love.

Thank you Cara Lyn! My girl! I'm so happy you found me on TikTok. Thank you for your passion for story, your kind words, and your amazing friendship. Looking forward to having some gluten free cupcakes and whiskey with you at some point in the future!

Thank you to every single blogger, book influencer, and reviewer who read and reviewed Wicked Midnight. I am in constant awe of your dedication and passion to sharing books with the world. Thank you for spending time with my characters and stories. My heart is full.

Thank you to my amazing editor Kat, of Kat's Literary Services. As always, you do such exceptional work. I feel like you really get what I'm trying to do.

Thank you to Maria at Artscandare Book Design for such a gorgeous cover. It perfectly encapsulates Wicked Midnight.

Thank you to Champagne Book Design for formatting Wicked Midnight. This is the seventh project I've worked on with you now and I can't imagine working with anyone else. You are the literal best in the biz.

Thank you to all of my friends and family. Whether you

know about this pen name or not, just being in my life is the best support I could ever get. Just existing is enough. I love each and every one of you.

And last but not least, thank you booktok. I found the best bookish family there with you all.

ABOUT THE AUTHOR

M Violet is a dark romance author with a flair for the dramatic. She likes whiskey, rainy nights, and writing by the fire. When she's not creating scorching hot villains for you to fall in love with, you can find her eating chocolate and binge watching her favorite shows.

Facebook: Authormviolet
Instagram: Authormviolet
Tik Tok: Authormviolet